Goosebumps

Haunted Halloween

Movie Novel

Goosebumps
Haunted Halloween

MOVIE NOVEL

EDITED AND INTRODUCED BY R.L. STINE
BASED ON THE MOTION PICTURE
WRITTEN BY ROB LIEBER

SCHOLASTIC INC.

GOOSEBUMPS and associated logos are registered trademarks of Scholastic Inc. © 2018 Columbia Pictures Industries, Inc. All Rights Reserved.

Published by Scholastic Inc., *Publishers since 1920*. SCHOLASTIC and associated logos are trademarks and/or registered trademarks of Scholastic Inc.

The publisher does not have any control over and does not assume any responsibility for author or third-party websites or their content.

ISBN 978-1-338-29957-1

10 9 8 7 6 5 4 3   18 19 20 21 22

Printed in the U.S.A.   40

First printing 2018

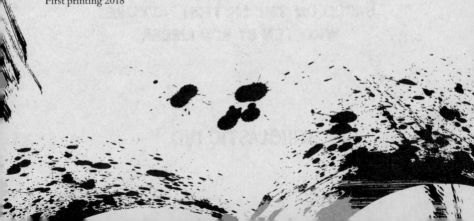

INTRODUCTION
R.L. STINE

How does Slappy, the evil dummy, celebrate Halloween?

By making sure no one else has a good time!

Sarah Quinn; her brother, Sonny; and his best friend, Sam, have made a terrible mistake. They have brought Slappy to life at Halloween time.

Sarah and the two boys are the only ones in town who know the dummy is alive. Alive and dangerous.

They try to get help to protect their friends—and the whole town—against him. But of course no one will believe them.

And why should they? We all know that wooden dummies can't come to life—*don't* we?

I really should apologize and take the blame for all the terrifying things that happen in this story. I admit that Slappy is my most evil creation—evil enough to star in his own movie.

In case you didn't know, the dummy was built by an evil sorcerer a few hundred years ago. The sorcerer used wood from a stolen coffin for Slappy's head. And he used his dark sorcery skills to give Slappy all kinds of nasty powers.

When the secret words are spoken, Slappy comes to life. He walks. He stalks. And trust me, he doesn't do good deeds.

In this story, Slappy gives everyone a Halloween to remember. Or, maybe a Halloween they wish they could forget! He doesn't terrify by himself—he brings to life every Halloween item he can find.

Jack-o'-lanterns, Halloween masks, costumes, skeletons, and other creepy decorations—he uses them all to frighten and destroy. (And . . . watch out for the most horrifying gummy bears that ever roared through a Halloween nightmare.)

Can Sarah, Sonny, and Sam save their town? Can they find a way to stop Slappy and all of the creatures he has enlisted in his army of trick-or-treat terror?

I won't spoil the fun for you. I'll just say this holiday will be a *scream*.

Slappy Halloween, everyone!

CHAPTER 1

Sarah Quinn knew about fear.

Fear is something that everyone experiences, she typed. *Fear is a feeling that we all know.*

The words unspooled across the bright white screen. Then, as Sarah tapped her finger furiously against the DELETE button, the whiteness swallowed them up.

Fear: a blank page.

Fear: a college essay, still to be written, the deadline getting closer by the minute.

Fear: all her plans, all her dreams, all her hopes of escaping this dull, familiar, small-town life—basically, her entire future—resting on this one, single essay. And she couldn't think of a single thing to write.

The application from Columbia University asked a seemingly simple question: *Write about a time when you faced a fear, challenge, or failure. How did it define you and how did you overcome it?*

Fear: getting rejected from Columbia. Losing the chance to pack her suitcase and take off for the big city, the one that sparkled brighter than the stars, the one that never slept.

Spending the rest of her life on Long Island, trapped in the shadow of the city that would never be hers. Spending the rest of her life in this dull split-level house, in this dull town, stuck in some dull, dead-end job, forever and ever and ever . . . Yes, Sarah Quinn knew plenty about fear. But she couldn't exactly write *that*.

For me, a fear that shaped my life was . . .

"That sucks," she told the screen, as if it was the computer's fault.

She pressed DELETE firmly and started from scratch yet again.

She drummed her fingers on the desk. Paced across the room and back again. Stood at the window, stared out at the night, waiting for inspiration to strike.

Not that there was any hope of that. This was Wardenclyffe, New York, the kind of quaint, boring town people moved to because they heard it was a safe place to raise their children.

Even tonight, a couple of days before Halloween, inflatable ghosts and goblins dancing on the roofs of the neighbors' houses, pumpkins grinning up from doorsteps with demonic grins, it was about the least scary place Sarah had ever seen.

Yes, looming in the distance was the shadowy silhouette of Wardenclyffe Lab, once the high-tech headquarters of the mad scientist Nikola Tesla, abandoned for more than a century. Yes, kids liked to ride their bikes out there, dare each other to ignore the giant KEEP OUT! signs and climb the barbed wire fence. Sarah had done it, too, when she was younger.

But that was kid stuff. She knew now there was nothing to be scared of at that lab, or probably anywhere else within a hundred miles.

Suddenly, she thought she caught a pair of eyes, gleaming in the darkness, staring back at her through the night. She blinked.

Just her imagination. Wishful thinking, maybe. She was just going to have to accept it: She lived a boring life in a boring place, and she would just have to make the best of it.

Sarah returned to the computer. Put her fingers on the keyboard. Stared. Waited. Didn't flinch at the sound of something scraping against the front of the house. Didn't stiffen at the soft patter that might have been feet climbing up the lattice toward her bedroom. Didn't worry about the whisper of wind that sounded like it was calling her name.

Until she heard a tapping at the window.

Sarah spun around. There was nothing there. She crept toward the window. "Hello?" she said. Nothing but darkness. Still . . .

Fear.

She crept closer, held her breath, then let it all out in a

sigh as she reached the window and confirmed she was alone with the night.

Alone, safe—until a ghoulish creature materialized in the darkness and slammed up against the glass.

Sarah screamed.

CHAPTER 2

The creature's mouth was fixed in a permanent howl. Its eyes burned white-hot. And its ratty T-shirt, with the logo of some band she'd never heard of, was familiar.

Sarah rolled her eyes and opened the window. "Tyler! What's wrong with you?"

Tyler was Sarah's boyfriend—or sort of boyfriend, or probably boyfriend? He didn't like labels, he always said.

He did, however, like Halloween.

Tyler climbed into Sarah's bedroom and pulled off his mask, still laughing. Despite herself, Sarah was laughing, too. This was the problem with Tyler. Even when he was annoying, which was often, he was still adorable.

"Are you crazy?" she asked in a hushed whisper. "My mom's gonna hear us!"

Sarah was seventeen; she was allowed to go on dates with boys. She was allowed to have a boyfriend, even the sort of probably kind. She was not, however, allowed to let boys crawl into her bedroom on a school night. Well, she'd

never exactly *asked* if she was allowed to do this. But she was pretty sure the answer would be a very loud, very angry *no*.

"Sorry, I was in the neighborhood," Tyler said, not sounding very sorry. "I texted you like ten times!"

"My phone's off," Sarah reminded him. "I told you if I miss this essay deadline, I don't get into college."

Tyler shrugged. College—like labels—was "not his thing." "Then you'll be here with me for the next four years. Consider me your safety school." He grinned charmingly. "Close by, good parties . . ."

Sarah suppressed a smile. "I'm looking for a more academic environment," she said, trying to sound serious. She wanted him to understand: This was important. Right now it was the most important thing of all. "With a solid creative writing department."

"I'm super creative!" Tyler said. "See, I brought you a care package." He pulled a crushed plastic bag out of his shirt. "Red Bull and Pringles."

"That's really sweet," Sarah said.

Tyler popped open the Pringles and crunched down on three at once. He'd bought his favorite flavor.

"I've never been so stuck in my life," Sarah complained. "I just keep deleting everything."

"Why don't you just copy an essay from the Internet?" Tyler suggested. There was a reason he had no plans to go to college.

Sarah sighed. It would take too long to explain to him all the things that were wrong with this suggestion. "Because it has to be personal," she said. "And *great*. And I don't know what I'm doing."

Tyler studied the application packet. "I'm here to help," he said, then read aloud, *"Write about a time in your life when you faced a fear, challenge, or failure."*

Sarah smiled at him. "When I had extreme writer's block and had to kick you out of my room before my mom came in . . ." she said, trying to sound like she meant it.

"Okay, fine, I'm going." Tyler stuck another fistful of chips into his mouth. "See you tomorrow."

She stopped him before he could get all the way out of the window. "Wait—I'll take the Red Bull. And the Pringles. And . . . thank you." She leaned in and took a bite of the stack of chips sticking out of his mouth. Their lips were only a breath apart.

She drew closer, about to kiss him good night, when the door swung open and Sarah's mother burst into the room. "You are so busted!" she cried.

CHAPTER 3

Kathy Quinn was wearing her bathrobe, which meant she must have already gone to bed. Sarah cringed. Her mother worked long shifts as a nurse at the local nursing home and never got enough sleep. There was nothing she hated more than being awakened.

"Soooo busted," Sonny echoed, peering around the doorway. Sarah's little brother held up his cell phone, to rub it in her face: He was videoing the whole thing. That was Sonny's latest annoying habit. He liked to record every embarrassing thing that happened to her, then share it with all his annoying little friends. "Sam is gonna love this." He hit SEND.

She would deal with him later. For now, she had a much bigger problem. "Mom, it's not what it looks like," she said.

"Tyler, go home," her mother said. Here was another thing that inspired fear in Sarah: her mother's voice, when it went all tight and quiet like that.

That was the sign she was biding her time, waiting to explode.

"Just to clarify, do you mean back out the window, or out the front door?" Tyler asked, grinning. Sarah wished she was psychic, so she could tell him via ESP that he should stop trying to charm her mother.

Kathy Quinn managed to tell him the same thing with a single look.

The grin dropped off Tyler's face. "I'll use the window. See you tomorrow, Sarah. Sorry."

"Mom, he was just dropping off a care package," Sarah said.

"Go to bed," her mother said, sounding tired. "We'll discuss this in the morning."

The next morning, Sonny Quinn achieved scientific greatness at his kitchen table. That was the plan, at least. He was putting the finishing touches on his science project, a perfect scale model of the Wardenclyffe Lab, with working electricity.

Except that the electricity wasn't exactly . . . working.

Sonny soldered the final wire, and—*zzzzap!* He yelped and dropped the soldering iron with a clatter.

It was just a tiny electric shock.

But it still hurt.

His mother, washing her breakfast dish at the sink, turned around with a look of only mild concern. "Hon, you need to stop electrocuting yourself and finish your breakfast. You need your energy."

"Mom, the only energy I need right now is for this Tesla coil to increase voltage AND amperage through the step-up transformer," Sonny complained. "My presentation is tomorrow, and it's fifty percent of my grade."

Sonny examined his model. He had built a tiny Tesla coil that was supposed to light up the laboratory's spindly tower. He was certain it would be the best project in the class. If he could only get it to work. One more try, he decided.

He plugged the coil into the outlet and turned it on. *Yes!* The tower sparked to life—

And, with an angry sizzle, shorted out the entire house.

"Sonny, seriously?" his mother asked wearily.

"Sorry!" Sonny said, undaunted. Tesla hadn't given up after his first try, or second, or, probably, his hundredth. Sonny wouldn't, either. "Scientific discovery requires experimentation."

Unfortunately, obnoxious big sisters didn't always understand that. Sarah barreled down the stairs with a flat iron in one hand and a fist of frizz in the other. "This is the fifth time this month you've blown the circuit breakers!"

Sonny swallowed his laughter. His sister looked ridiculous with her hair half-straightened. But even he knew better than to point it out. Sarah opened the box and reset the circuit breakers. The lights came back on.

"Just put your hair up," Kathy advised. "I have to run an errand on the way to school and we're already late!"

Sarah grumbled, shot Sonny a nasty look, then tromped up the stairs to finish getting ready.

The doorbell rang, and Sonny jumped up. Finally!

His best friend, Sam, stood on the doorstep, backpack slung over his shoulder and a duffel bag at his feet.

"Morning, Mrs. Quinn," he chirped.

Sam spent almost as much time at the Quinn house as Sonny did, but this week, he was moving in while his parents went on some incredibly boring vacation to the countryside. It was perfect timing: Halloween was coming up fast. Now he and Sonny would have plenty of time to work on their costumes, their jack-o'-lanterns, and their candy-hoarding strategies. Sonny couldn't wait.

Sam's father was still in the car, idling at the curb. He waved through the open window. "Kathy, thanks so much for taking Sam!" he called to Sonny's mother. "He has our contact info at the hotel. We'll be back in three days. We owe you!"

"You definitely do," Sonny's mother said. Her voice was sweet, but it sounded like she meant it.

Sam dumped his stuff in the corner. Sonny's mom scooped up everything she needed for work, tossing it into her bag. "Sonny! Backpack on now," she said, then called upstairs. "Sarah, let's go!"

Sarah bounded down, her hair pulled into a loose ponytail, now looking only a tiny bit ridiculous.

"My condolences about your bust last night," Sam told her. "Good thing I'll be here for a few nights to keep you safe if any other dudes climb in your window."

For the second time that morning, Sonny swallowed a laugh. For reasons Sonny could not fathom, Sam worshipped Sarah. He always had. He was convinced that someday, Sarah would notice his great devotion and reward him for it.

Sonny didn't have the nerve to tell his friend that Sarah thought of him like a particularly persistent mosquito. He should just be grateful he hadn't been squashed yet.

Sarah glared at Sonny. She *hated* it when he filmed her getting in trouble. Which only made it more fun to do. "Sonny, I'm going to kill you."

"Kill him in the car," their mother said, ushering them all out the door. "We're late."

Sonny waved at their neighbor, Mr. Chu, who was out in his yard working on his Halloween decorations. Mr. Chu was *very* into Halloween and had been working on these decorations for the entire month.

Every year, he made a bigger and bigger display. Sonny gasped at the sight of it. This year, like every year, his yard was covered with cardboard goblins, witches, trolls, and ghosts.

But while Sonny was asleep, Mr. Chu had added something new: a gigantic, two-story spider scaling his roof. It

looked almost real, except it was made almost entirely out of black balloons. Sonny shuddered. He hated spiders.

"Wow, you've practically got a theme park going this year," Sonny's mother said.

"You know it," Mr. Chu said cheerfully. He was taping together another leg for the giant roof spider. "Wait till you see my costumes . . . with an *S*. I've got more than one, is what I'm saying."

Sonny's mother smiled. "Very impressive."

"Hey, check this out!" Mr. Chu said. He pressed a button on the remote control, and the spider's leg lifted a couple inches. It was . . . not as impressive as he seemed to think. "It moves! Gonna have this puppy up and running for Halloween." He cleared his throat. "Uh, for the kids, you know."

Sam waited until they were safely in the car before asking, "He doesn't actually have kids, does he?"

"No," Sonny's mother confirmed. "He does not."

Before school, they stopped at Walgreens so Sonny's mother could pick up a prescription for one of her patients. She told Sam and Sonny they could each pick a pumpkin to carve.

Sam, however, had other ideas. He pulled Sonny to the front of the store, where there was a large bulletin board crowded with handmade flyers. They advertised babysitters, apartments for rent, lawn mowers, tutors, bikes for sale—it seemed like anything a person could have or need was somewhere on this board. Sam tacked up a giant flyer of his own, right at the center.

Need someone to pick up your junk? it read. *Call THE JUNK BROS—the best in junk removal.*

Sam was a businessman, or at least, that's how he liked to think of himself. He was always coming up with a new get-rich-quick scheme—and always persuading Sonny to jump on board. Junk Bros was his newest scheme. Sonny was skeptical. Also slightly embarrassed.

"Really?" he said. It hadn't occurred to him the flyer would go up where people he knew might actually *see* it. "Here?"

"Yes, here," Sam said. "Everywhere. It's called marketing."

Mission accomplished, they set off to pick out some pumpkins.

"Why do you insist on calling us brothers?" Sonny asked. "It feels like fraud."

"'Cause we're basically brothers," Sam said. "And studies show that four out of five consumers trust family-owned businesses more than corporations."

"Where did you read that?"

Sam shrugged. "I didn't. I made it up. But if you make a point and back it up with a 'study,' no one can argue with it. Seventy-eight percent of all people know that."

Sometimes it was useful to have a best friend who had an argument for everything.

Often, though, it was just exhausting.

CHAPTER 4

Sarah followed her mother through the drugstore aisles as she picked up various supplies for the nursing home. Sarah felt like she could hear a clock ticking down. Any minute now—

"Something you want to say to me?" her mother said.

Finally. It was almost a relief. "Mom, I was working all night, I swear," Sarah said quickly. "Tyler just snuck over and I've been so stuck on this essay, I just . . ."

"Because you're getting distracted," Kathy said sharply. Then she softened. She was the only one who really understood how much this mattered to Sarah. "You're a great writer, Sarah. You always have been. You just need to trust yourself."

"It's just really hard to write about facing fears and defining moments when I live in a town where nothing ever happens! And when you try to sum up your whole life in one essay, it all sounds so . . . unimpressive."

Kathy stopped short in the aisle and turned to face her daughter. She used her serious voice, the one that said *you better listen to this.* "Honey, you're top of your class. Editor of the literary magazine. You've done all that while helping take care of the house and your brother these last few years." Her eyes were shining with pride. "You're the most impressive girl I know."

"You really think so?" Sarah said. Her mother never talked like this.

"I do . . . which is why I need you to watch Sonny and Sam this week while I work doubles."

Sarah's heart sank. Of course her mother was just buttering her up so she could sucker Sarah into free babysitting. "Are you kidding, Mom?" she whined. "My essay's due Friday."

Her mother looked satisfied. "And now you'll be home all week to finish it without distractions."

Checkmate.

"Sonny's thirteen!" Sarah protested, though she already knew it wouldn't help. "He's old enough to watch himself."

"Have you seen what he blows up when he's supervised? Imagine what he's capable of wrecking when he's *unsupervised.*"

"Mom . . ."

"Hon, I know you're focused on getting out of here," her mother said. This was true, and this kind of thing was exactly why! "But right now, you're still here with us. And I need to know I can count on you—"

"Yeah, fine." Sarah couldn't stand to let her mother finish the guilt trip. Not when she'd spent the last three years doing *everything* her mother asked of her. Of course she knew she could count on Sarah! And that was the problem, of course. Sarah was the kind of girl you could count on. Sarah did exactly what she was asked to do. So her mother kept asking.

Just then, Sam and Sonny showed up, pushing a cart heaped with pumpkins and gummy bears.

"Pumpkins were on sale," Sonny explained, before anyone could ask.

"What's with all the candy?" their mother said skeptically. "Is *that* on sale?"

Sam shook his head. "But, Mrs. Quinn, *that* is an investment in your Halloween experience. You will not be sorry. Gummy bears put smiles on people's faces. Which makes your house a 'good candy' house. Which elevates your status in the community. Studies show—"

Sarah and her mother rolled their eyes in sync. Her mother put the candy back on the shelf, and they approached the register together.

Standing behind the counter was the most handsome man Sarah had ever seen in Wardenclyffe. Which, granted, wasn't saying much. But still, he was very good-looking for a guy her mom's age. And when Sarah's mother said hello like she knew him, he started blushing.

19

"Hey, Kathy, you're looking nice this morning," he said.

Sarah's mother tugged at her nursing scrubs. "This old thing?" she teased. "I hear blue is in."

Sarah couldn't believe it. Was her mother actually . . . *flirting*?

Gross.

The guy laughed. His name was Walter, according to his name tag. He scanned their purchases, then paused on the last one. "The adult diapers are two for one, if you want to grab another," he suggested.

Sarah's mother flushed bright red. "No!" she practically shouted. "One package is all I need. For work! Not for me!"

Sarah almost groaned. Her mother had literally no game.

"Okay, see you soon," Walter said, handing her the receipt. Then added, with a bashful smile, "Hopefully . . ."

"You know it," Kathy said eagerly. "Thanks for checking me out!" Then she must have realized how that sounded, because she blushed even brighter. "I mean, uh, checking me out." She pointed to the register. "Not 'checking me out.'"

Sarah dragged her mother out of the store before things could get any more awkward. "Smooth, Mom," she teased. "Very smooth."

Sam stopped cold in the center of the busiest hallway in Daniel Webster Middle School. "Perfect," he murmured, then slapped a Junk Bros flyer up on the wall.

"Hey, science fair sign-ups!" Sonny said, checking out the flyer next to Sam's on the bulletin board. "If I can get my Tesla Tower to work, I can win this year. That would be so cool."

"Sonny, we're already cool. We're treasure hunters," Sam countered. "People respect us. They—"

Thwap! A soaked spit wad smacked Sam in the face.

Sonny didn't think that was the kind of respect his best friend had in mind.

The two boys turned around slowly. They didn't have to look to know who would be standing behind them, spit ball straws in hand, goony grins on their faces.

"Hey, Junk Bros!" It was Tommy Madigan and his eighth-grade goon squad. "If you're looking for junk, there's some standing right here in this hallway."

"Sorry, we don't have a wagon big enough to cart you away," Sam jeered.

Tommy stopped laughing. A beat later, his lackeys fell silent, too.

"What did you say?" he asked, taking a step toward them. Tommy was big. And he liked to break things. Things like puny seventh graders who insulted him.

"What are you doing?" Sonny asked his best friend in a low, worried voice.

"We were gonna TP Principal Harrison's house tomorrow night," Tommy said, moving so close that Sonny could smell his breath. Onions and orange juice. Sonny tried not to gag. "But now I think I'm just gonna spend the whole night chasing you guys around."

Tommy poked Sonny's chest so sharply that Sonny stumbled backward.

Lucky for him, a teacher showed up just in time. "Boys! Move it or you're tardy."

Tommy immediately turned to her and said politely, "Of course, Mrs. Hoover. I was just extolling my deep love of homework and all things learning to my good friend Sonny here."

Mrs. Hoover rolled her eyes. "Uh . . . sure. Well, get to class."

Sonny and Sam scurried in one direction. Tommy and his goons thumped off in another. But Sonny was still seething. "Someday, that jerk is going to get a taste of his own medicine," he muttered to Sam.

CHAPTER 5

Sarah was sitting in the school library with her nose in a book when someone slid another book across the counter toward her. She looked up expectantly.

Tyler grinned back at her. "I'd like to check this book out, please."

Sarah scanned his ID. "Hmmm, unfortunately you have four books that haven't been returned since your sophomore year. Which I'm guessing is the last time you were in a library. So your account is frozen. It'll cost forty bucks to unfreeze it."

Tyler sighed. "Darn. I just spent that on tickets for the show at the Den tonight."

Sarah looked up in surprise. "Really?"

Tyler grinned. "It's my way of saying sorry for getting you busted last night. You need to come. Don't say no. Consider it a date."

A date! They never went on actual *dates*. Sarah's heart leaped—and then sailed right off a cliff as she remembered

23

that she couldn't go anywhere that night, concert or no concert.

"I can't," she told him. "My mom's making me watch my idiot brother and his friend all week."

Tyler tipped his head toward the low-slung couches, where a bunch of his friends were lounging and playing on their phones.

"Guys, tell Sarah to come."

Without looking up from their phones, they did as he asked.

"You should come."

"Yeah, totally."

"Don't be lame."

"See?" Tyler said. "You're wanted."

Sarah doubted that. She wasn't exactly friends with Tyler's friends. In fact, most of the time, they pretended she didn't even exist. But it was clear that *Tyler* wanted her there, and that was all she cared about.

Still. "I have to finish my essay," she said, trying to convince herself.

"Come on, don't wait till next year to have some fun," he wheedled. Tyler was good at getting what he wanted. "Show starts at eight. Get your brother a babysitter."

Sarah told him she'd think about it, and for the rest of the day, she did—obsessively. She couldn't defy her mother and ditch her brother. Of course she couldn't.

Could she?

24

Sonny put the finishing touch on his jack-o'-lantern and set down the knife. He inspected his work: perfect. He'd carved the large pumpkin to make it look like it was eating a smaller pumpkin. It was exactly the right balance of spooky and disgusting. He looked over to see how Sam's pumpkin was doing.

Sam's pumpkin looked as if its face had caved in.

"Dude, you're so good at this," Sam said, enviously.

"You have to take your time," Sonny advised him. "I feel like each pumpkin has its own spirit. You have to listen to the pumpkin. Let it tell you what it wants to be."

Sam looked intently at his pumpkin. "Okay. If I'm hearing you correctly, you want me to give you a mouth," he said. He began carving.

Soon there was a big, gaping hole where a mouth should be. "All right, that worked."

The boys were still laughing when Sarah came in to the kitchen. She grabbed a soda, then came over to check out their work. "Not bad," she said.

Sam preened. "Thanks. It's a spiritual exercise. You let the pumpkin guide your carving—"

"I was talking about Sonny's," Sarah said. "Yours looks like it was carved by a seven-year-old." She scooped up a handful of pumpkin guts and tossed them at Sam.

"Don't you have an essay to write?" he said sulkily.

"Yeah, so I'll be in my room," she told them. "You two are on your own. Just don't mess anything up."

She was barely out of the kitchen before Sam's cell rang. He answered and, after a few seconds, his face lit up. "Yes, you're speaking to a Junk Bro," he told whoever was calling. "This afternoon? Hmm . . ." There was a dramatic pause. "We're pretty booked today. Let me check with my associate."

Sonny shook his head. They still had five more pumpkins to carve. The last thing he wanted to do with his afternoon was—

"You're in luck," Sam told the caller, and flashed Sonny a thumbs-up. "We can squeeze you in!"

He hung up the phone, triumphant. "Get your shoes on," he told Sonny. "It's time to get rich!"

They rode their bikes, their Junk Bros wagons trailing behind them.

Sam hit the brakes in front of an old, decaying house at the end of a long, cracked driveway. Its gray paint was peeling. Its windows were broken and boarded up. Its shadow cast them in cool darkness. It looked like no one had lived there for years, and Sonny could see why.

"Twenty-four Ashley Lane," Sam said, double-checking the address. "I guess this is it."

"Twenty-four is probably the number of people who

were murdered here," Sonny said. But they'd taken the job. They had no choice but to go inside.

A cluster of garden gnomes dotted the lawn. Sonny knew he was being silly, but he felt like their painted eyes were tracking his movements. "I don't like the way those things are looking at us," he complained.

"Treasure hunters, remember," Sam said.

Sonny tried to steel himself. They weren't little kids anymore, right? He knew better than to believe in things like haunted houses.

He raised a hand, hesitantly, and tapped at the door. It opened with an ominous creak. Sam swiped a gigantic cobweb out of the way and stepped inside. Sonny forced himself to follow, but he wasn't happy about it.

He *really* hated spiders.

The house was a dump. Heaps of old mattresses and ratty couches were piled in the shadowy living room. There were broken lamps, boxes of moldy files, cracked dishes, faded blankets. All junk—no treasure.

At the far end of the room, a large marble fireplace took up almost the entire wall. A sheet-covered pile loomed in front of it. Anything could be under there.

Money.

Treasure.

Bodies.

"Come on, it's not so bad," Sam said. Sonny could hear him trying to keep the nervousness out of his voice. Sam reached for the sheet, steeling himself to yank it away. "There is literally nothing to be afraid of."

He tugged at the sheet, which dropped to reveal a gigantic cat, its fur midnight black, its eyes gleaming viciously, its claws razor sharp.

And it was lunging straight for them.

CHAPTER 6

Sonny and Sam screamed, the noise echoing through the empty house.

The cat didn't flinch.

Actually, the cat didn't move at all.

The cat was nailed to a wooden base on the fireplace, stiff and stuffed, and no threat to anyone. Not anymore.

Sonny drew in a deep breath, feeling a little silly and a lot relieved.

"How much are they paying us for this?" he asked Sam.

Sam looked sheepish.

"Sam?" Sonny pressed. He had a sudden bad feeling. "Tell me we're getting paid *something*."

"It's not for *free*," Sam said quickly. "The lady on the phone said we can keep any junk we don't throw away. Some of this stuff could have monetary value."

"You know what else has monetary value? Actual money."

Disgusted, Sonny turned his back on his friend and started hauling the junk out to the trash bins on the side of the house. It was hard, sweaty, boring work.

Work no one was paying for.

It seemed to take forever. But finally, the house was empty except for a couple cardboard boxes of all the "treasure" they planned to take with them: One fan. Three doorknobs. One rusty trophy.

"How's that for actual money?" Sam said, patting a box proudly like it contained a pirate's bounty. Sonny suppressed the urge to dump it out on his head.

Sonny remembered the dead, stuffed cat and thought they might as well take that, too. At the very least, he could use it to freak out his sister. He grabbed the cat, but it wouldn't move. It was stuck on something. He pulled harder. The cat twisted on the platform, and something deep beneath it started clicking and groaning.

A moment later, the back of the fireplace slid open.

"Whoa," the boys breathed together. A secret passageway? Maybe there was something worth *something* in this house after all.

They crouched down and peered into the dark, dusty nook behind the fireplace. Sam pulled out a heavy wooden crate and immediately set to work trying to pry it open. "Dude, I bet this thing is stuffed with gold and diamonds and bitcoins—"

"Bitcoins are a crypto-currency," Sonny corrected him. "They're not actual coins, they're *virtual* coins. See, it starts with a process known as mining, and then—"

"Can you stop being a nerd for one second and help me?" Sam said.

"Right . . . sorry," Sonny said. Together they yanked at the lid and, finally, the crate popped open. They looked inside, eager to claim their reward.

There was nothing in there except a dusty old leather-bound book.

"Well, that was disappointing," said Sam.

Sonny pulled out the book and gave it a closer look. "It's locked."

Sure enough, the book was shut tight with a lock.

A lock that seemed exactly the right size for the key that lay at the bottom of the box.

"Here, try this," said Sam, grabbing the key.

Sonny opened it.

"So, what's in it?"

Sonny flipped through the manuscript pages, all of them covered with fading ink. "Just some beat-up old book. It doesn't even have a title."

"The cover could probably get us a few bucks," Sam suggested, and tossed the book into one of the boxes.

Sonny went to put the lid back on the crate, then jerked his hand back. "Uh, Sam? Turn around," he said nervously.

Sam looked over at the box. Sitting inside, grinning up at them with a creepy red smile, was a wooden ventriloquist dummy. It wore a gray suit and a red bow tie. "That wasn't there before, was it?"

Sonny could swear it had *not* been inside the box the first time they looked.

That was impossible, of course.

It *had* to be.

A scrap of paper poked out of the dummy's suit pocket. Sonny read aloud, *"Hi. My name's Slappy. What's yours?"* He grinned at the dummy. "Sonny and Sam." Maybe the little doll wasn't so creepy after all. Maybe it would even be worth something.

"There's more writing on the back," Sam said.

Sonny flipped the paper over. Sam was right, but the words didn't make any sense to him. *"Karru Marri Odonna Loma Molonu Karrano,"* he read out loud. "I think it's some sort of foreign language?"

Slappy just sat there, smiling his frozen smile, like he was waiting for them to do something. Or like he was *hoping* for it.

"So creepy," Sam said, tapping the doll's wooden hair. "He looks alive."

Sonny looked around at the living room's peeling paint and broken windows.

There was nothing but dust, rust, and spiderwebs. He wondered what kind of person would live in a creepy house like this. What kind of person would leave all his stuff behind, including a creepy dummy and a dead cat. "I don't think anything's been alive in this house since that cat," he said.

"Guess what," a low, menacing voice said from behind him. Sonny's heart thumped wildly in his chest. He whirled around and came face-to-face with Slappy the dummy. *"I'm alive now!"*

CHAPTER 7

"Hey, Sonny, give me a kiss!" the dummy begged. Slappy's face was close enough to take a bite out of him.

And cackling madly, right behind the dummy's face, was Sam. He waved the dummy at Sonny. "Just one smooch, right on the lips!"

Sonny shook off his raw terror. He would have to pretend he hadn't been afraid, or Sam would never let him live it down. "What is *wrong* with you?" he snapped.

"You should have seen your face." Sam was laughing so hard he could barely speak. "Afraid of a puppet."

"Whatever," Sonny said. "I wasn't scared."

He couldn't blame Sam for laughing. Who would be afraid of a little wooden doll?

They'd loaded their booty into their wagons and were almost ready to ride back home when trouble rolled up on a bike of his own. Trouble with a capital T, and that spelled Tommy Madigan. Of course, he had his goon squad with him.

Sonny wondered if they ever went anywhere without Tommy. Probably they'd be completely clueless without the big bully telling them what to do.

"Hey, it's the Junk Sisters," Tommy jeered.

"At least we know our marketing's working?" Sam whispered to Sonny.

Sonny just glared at him. This had already been the worst afternoon of his week and it had just taken a pretty sharp nosedive.

"No teacher around to save you now," Tommy said.

Sonny felt his heart thumping again. He'd never been in an actual fight. And he didn't especially want that to change.

Tommy gave Sonny a weird look. "Hey, are you wearing my old sweater? From my grandma's yard sale?" He walked around Sonny in a slow circle, taking him in from all sides.

Sonny wanted to disappear. He begged his mother not to make him wear hand-me-down clothes, but she said they were just as good as new.

There was nothing good about this.

"Is that why you call yourself the Junk Bros?" Tommy laughed. "'Cause you wear other people's junk?"

"Leave us alone," Sam said, in the voice he used when he wanted to sound tough.

But he's not tough, Sonny thought, ashamed of himself for thinking it. *Neither of us are.*

Tommy looked like he was trying to make a decision. His face furrowed in deep thought. Maybe he didn't have a

lot of practice at thinking. Finally, he said, "Give me my sweater back and I'll let you go."

"Really?" Sonny couldn't believe anyone would be that petty and mean.

"Unless you want your face punched."

Sonny very much did not want his face punched. "Fine."

He took off his sweater. It felt filthy, now that he knew it had once belonged to Tommy. He hated this sweater, hated his mother for making him wear it, hated Tommy for making him feel like garbage, hated Tommy's thugs and even Sam for being there to watch.

Mostly, though, he hated himself for doing exactly what Tommy told him to. For being afraid to do anything else.

"And the box," Tommy said, pointing at the box with the manuscript and the dead cat.

"Whatever." Sonny was now in only an undershirt. He just wanted to get home and forget this day had ever happened. What did he care about some old book and a dead cat?

Tommy knelt and started going through the box. "Let's see. Stupid book. Doorknobs. Wow, great business you guys are running. Oh—cool." He'd found the cat. "This is actually awesome." Then he turned to Sam. "Your turn."

"I'm not giving you my box," Sam said stubbornly.

"Come on, man," Sonny said quietly. Why did Sam have to make everything harder than it had to be? "I like my face un-punched."

"No way! We worked for this stuff," Sam insisted.

Tommy reached into the box and grabbed Slappy.

"Dude, give him back!" Sam shouted, reaching for the dummy.

Tommy held Slappy out of Sam's reach. The goon squad laughed and laughed. "Oh, you want your doll?" Tommy taunted him in a singsong voice. "Are you gonna dress him up when you get home?"

Sonny couldn't look at the ugly sneer on Tommy's face for one more second, and he also couldn't stand to look at poor Sam, jumping and lunging at the doll that Tommy kept yanking away from him at the last second. So instead, his eyes landed on Slappy's face. Which somehow seemed no longer to be smiling. It was impossible, but Sonny could swear that Slappy's face had twisted into a cruel sneer, mirroring Tommy's.

At that moment, Tommy's pants dropped to his ankles, exposing Tweety Bird boxers.

Sam and Sonny locked eyes. Then they burst into laughter.

"What the—" Red-faced, Tommy yanked up his pants, which stayed up for a second, then dropped once again to his ankles. Now his goon squad was pointing and laughing at *him*.

As Tommy struggled with his mysteriously mischievous pants, Sam yanked Slappy out of Tommy's grip and shoved him *hard* against his bike. Tommy stumbled backward into a heap, bike and boy tangled together.

Sonny looked at his best friend in horrified awe.

Sam grinned and hopped on his bike. "Go!"

They went.

Fast as they could, pedaling faster than they'd ever pedaled before, Tommy and the others soon hot on their trail. They gunned it down Ashley Lane, made a sharp left on Maple, sped past block after block, but Sonny could feel the junk wagons slowing them down. Tommy and his crew were steadily gaining.

Sonny risked a glance over his shoulder to see how close they were, but again, his gaze caught on Slappy, lying in the wagon.

Did the dummy just wink at him?

As they passed the next front yard, a garden hose uncoiled itself, shot across the street, and clotheslined Tommy and the goon squad in a single, efficient blow. All four of them flew from their bikes and slammed down onto the concrete.

Sam and Sonny skidded to a stop, gaping at the bruised and groaning pile of bullies.

"What happened?" Sam asked in amazement.

Sonny glanced at the doll—still motionless and limp in the wagon. Of course it was, he told himself. What else would a wooden doll be doing?

"I don't know," he said. But he wondered.

When they made it home safe and sound, Tommy and

the goons far behind, Sam gave Sonny a high five. "Maybe it was Slappy," Sam suggested. "He's our good luck charm."

It wasn't you, Sonny said silently to the doll, carrying it into the house. *It couldn't have been.*

Slappy's smile was fixed on his face again, smug and knowing, as if to say, *That's what you think.*

CHAPTER 8

Sarah's mother had left her a to-do list.

As if babysitting two bratty boys wasn't enough.

Fold laundry. Make boys dinner. Take out recycling. Help Sonny with science. Finish your essay. Her mother had drawn a smiley face at the bottom.

Sarah didn't smile.

Sam and Sonny burst through the doors, laughing and babbling about something involving a garden hose and a doll. Sarah didn't bother to listen, because it sounded ridiculous and knowing them it surely was.

They didn't seem to notice that she didn't care.

"Sarah, you have to hear what happened!" Sonny said exuberantly. "We were at this creepy house on Ashley Lane and the fireplace opened up and—"

"We found this secret compartment," Sam cut in, "and long story short, we found *this* guy—" Sam waved a creepy wooden ventriloquist dummy in the air proudly, as if it was some precious work of art.

"Wow, it's like you're actively trying not to be cool," Sarah said. She could not *believe* she was home making conversation about some crappy old house while Tyler and his friends were at a concert. "There's pizza in the oven," she told them. "Should be enough for you and your wooden friend. Oh, and—" She scooped up the pile of clothes her mother had left for her. "Here you go. Mom specifically said you should fold the laundry. I'll be working in my room if you need me. But, *do not* need me."

Sarah left the boys to their dinner and shut herself in her room to work on her essay.

Two hours later, she was still staring at the same blinking cursor and the same blank page. She checked Instagram, just to torture herself with how much fun everyone else was having.

Specifically, how much fun Tyler was having at the concert. Judging from the photos: a lot.

She could have been there with him. She *should* have been there with him.

But no, instead: Laundry. Babysitting. Essay.

Recount a time when you faced a fear, challenge, or failure.

How about the time I realized my whole life might be passing me by, Sarah thought. What was she doing? What could it hurt, just once, to have a little fun?

It only took a few minutes to toss on something suitable for a concert and hastily swipe on some lipstick and mascara.

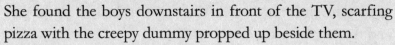

She found the boys downstairs in front of the TV, scarfing pizza with the creepy dummy propped up beside them.

"I'm out of here," she said, trying to sound casual about it.

"Where are you going?" Sonny asked, sounding extremely un-casual.

"Checking out a concert with Tyler. I'll be back by ten. If Mom calls, tell her I'm in the shower."

"But Mom said you were gonna help me practice my science presentation tonight!"

Sarah felt a brief stab of guilt. It wasn't her brother's fault that she was always stuck babysitting him, or that their mother refused to believe he was old enough to take care of himself.

On the other hand, it wasn't Sarah's fault, either. And if she stayed here and did what she was supposed to do, what would her reward be? Yet another to-do list. She told herself her brother would be fine. He always was.

"There's two dummies on the couch," she said. "Practice on one of them."

Sarah had never been to the Den Theater before, but when she got there, she was surprised to see it wasn't much like a theater at all. More like a small club, swarming with people who all dressed like Tyler did. They all seemed older than her, and cooler, and like they knew exactly what to do and who to talk to.

Sarah reminded herself that she just had to find Tyler, and then everything would be fine.

Inside, the club thumped with music. It was sweaty and crowded, a mass of people bouncing and shaking in time to the heavy bass line. Sarah just wanted to find Tyler. She checked her phone, hoping to text him: no service.

She had no choice but to find him the old-fashioned way. She threaded through the crowd, scanning faces. Dancers bumped and jostled her, and most of the time, they didn't even notice. She started to feel like she was invisible.

And then, finally, she spotted Tyler's familiar grin across the room. She smiled and stood on her tiptoes, waving at him over the crowd. He couldn't see her in the mass of people, so she started pushing her way toward him. He was going to be so surprised to see her here.

And so was his date.

Sarah stopped short as a slender, beautiful girl wrapped her arms around Tyler's neck. Sarah recognized her from school—a junior named Jess, who'd always been particularly unfriendly to her. Now Sarah understood why.

Jess brushed her lips against Tyler's ear. He seemed to like it. Sarah felt like she was going to throw up. She told herself to look away.

She could not look away.

Tyler tipped his face toward Jess's perfect, glossy lips. They kissed.

The music pounded. The dancers thrashed. Sarah felt like she was standing inside a frozen cone of silence, untouched, untouchable.

She had never felt so alone.

Sam was getting better at pumpkin carving . . . slightly. His newest masterpiece was a soldier pumpkin, complete with an army hat on its head. "I will call you Sergeant Squash," he said proudly.

Sonny left him to his work. He had a science presentation to prepare for, and his sister had turned out to be useless. As usual. He needed an audience to practice on, and since Sam was incapable of staying silent for more than thirty seconds in a row, he wasn't an option.

Instead, Sonny propped Slappy up on his bed. The dummy grinned at him. Sonny grinned back. Then he shuffled his note cards, took a deep breath, and began.

"It was more than one hundred years ago when the residents of Wardenclyffe, New York, looked out their windows to see strange lights streaking across the sky. But it wasn't Mother Nature lighting up the sky. It was Nikola Tesla!"

Sonny called up the first slide in his PowerPoint presentation, a portrait of Nikola Tesla. It was upside down.

"Sorry. Still working out the kinks," he told Slappy while he tweaked the slide. "Okay. So. Tesla wanted to create a world where anything could be transmitted through giant

43

electric towers: power, sound, maybe even brain waves. It was like the original Wi-Fi."

Sonny looked up to see how his audience was doing. Slappy seemed to be listening carefully.

"But he mysteriously shut down his lab in 1908. His tower never lit the sky again. Until today! When I will light this light bulb from across the room using a *real-life* Tesla coil inside this tower."

Sonny set the light bulb carefully in Slappy's lap. Then he took the two wires feeding out of the tower and touched them together. There was a bright spark!

But no light in the light bulb.

The experiment was a failure yet again.

"Come on, can this work just once?" Sonny muttered, frustrated. He walked himself through each step, checking that he'd done everything he was supposed to: adjust the gain on the amplifier circuit, kick up the AC voltage to fifty megahertz, and . . .

He brought the two wires together again. *"Voilà!"*

Another spark, an electric zap shooting through his fingertips. No light. Sonny looked apologetically up at the poster hanging over his bed: a portrait of Nikola Tesla. The scientist seemed to be glowering at him, disappointed.

"Don't give me that look," Sonny said. "I'm trying to bring your tower back to life."

At least the dummy wasn't judging him, he thought—at the exact moment the dummy turned his head.

All by himself.

And opened his mouth. *"Bravo,"* Slappy said. *"I, for one, think it's an* electrifying *presentation."*

"I'm not falling for that one again, Sam," Sonny said, impressed that his friend had managed to figure out a way to rig the dummy to talk from so far away. He examined Slappy, trying to figure out how Sam had pulled it off. It was a cool trick, he could admit that much.

"What is there, like, a mic?" Sonny pried Slappy's mouth open and spoke directly into it. "And you're talking through your cell phone? Nice try, dude. Totally not scared."

That's when the wooden dummy raised its wooden hands and pushed Sonny to the floor. *"You brought me to life,"* Slappy rasped. *"Don't you remember, Sonny?"*

Sonny went cold all over. No way could Sam have rigged this. But the other option was . . . not an option.

"How are you speaking to me right now?" Sonny asked in a choked voice.

Slappy smiled. There was a cruel, greedy gleam in his wooden eyes. *"I've always wanted a brother!"*

45

CHAPTER 9

Sonny scooted away from the dummy. Then he backed out of the room and slammed the door shut between them.

He was going nuts.

That was the only possible explanation.

"Sam!" he shouted, trying not to let his panic consume him. He was a scientist, right? There was a rational explanation for this—there had to be. He just had to find it. "*Sam! Get in here!*"

"Dude, I told you, I don't care about Tesla!" Sam called up the stairs.

Sonny was afraid to let his bedroom door out of his sight. He was afraid if he did, it might open. And something might come out of it.

Sam came upstairs, looking none too happy about it. "Please don't try to educate me about electricity—" His voice broke off abruptly as Sonny swung the door open and revealed Slappy, standing in the middle of the bedroom, all by himself.

"*Hello, Sam,*" the dummy said. "*Thank you for saving me from that moron today.*"

"Whoa," Sam exclaimed. "Is he battery-operated or something?"

Sonny felt a gush of relief. If Sam could see it, too, that meant he wasn't going crazy.

On the other hand, it also meant . . .

"He's alive!" Sonny said.

Sam closed in on Slappy to get a better look, but Slappy backed out of his reach. Sam's eyes nearly bugged out of his head.

"Sorry for what happened to Tommy, but I guess you could say he got . . . hosed." Slappy laughed at his own joke.

Sonny gaped. "That was *you?*"

"Yep." The dummy cackled. *"And now that we're family, we can be brothers. In fact, I think I'd make a great Junk Bro."*

Sam and Sonny exchanged nervous glances. "Uh, conference?" Sam suggested.

They turned their backs on the dummy and huddled together.

"Are we losing our minds?" Sam whispered.

"I don't think we can both lose our minds at the same time," Sonny said, as quietly as he could. "Maybe he's real."

"Of course I'm real!" Slappy said brightly. He was, somehow, standing right in front of them. *"And I can make your problems go away. Didn't your sister tell you to fold the laundry?"* He swiveled his wooden head toward the pile of clothes that Sonny had brought upstairs earlier.

They folded themselves.

48

"There. Now you have time to do your homework." Slappy winked. *"Oh, what's that? You don't want to do homework? That's okay, I just did it for you!"*

Sam and Sonny whirled around to discover a pen scribbling its way across Sonny's notebook. Sam grabbed the notebook off the desk and discovered a page of math work, fully completed.

"You know *algebra*?" Sam said in disbelief.

"Someone's getting an A-plus," Slappy said gleefully.

"Whoa." Sam had a look in his eye that Sonny recognized all too well. It was the look of a scheme. "Can you change *all* of our grades?"

"I can only affect the things in front of me," Slappy said. *"But whatever I see, I can bring to life."* His eyes closed as he recited the strange incantation they'd found in his pocket. *"Karru Marri Odonna Loma Molonu Karrano . . ."*

Sonny held his breath.

A moment later, a pile of old action figures twitched and rolled, then picked themselves up and waved at Sonny. He waved back in awe. "Sam, I will never question collecting junk again. Wait till Sarah and my mom see this."

Slappy's eyes flew open, and as they did, the action figures dropped to the ground. Life drained out of them.

"Let's keep this our little secret, for now," Slappy said.

Sonny felt the chill of goosebumps rising on his neck. There was something in the dummy's voice, something that left him uneasy.

"Give me a chance to win them over first," Slappy added, and Sonny realized what was worrying him.

The way Slappy said it—it wasn't a request.

It was an order.

After Sarah had seen Tyler with Jess, there was no point in staying at the concert. She'd walked out, half hoping that Tyler would notice her just in time and come after her. Say something, anything, to explain away what he'd done.

He didn't.

Of course he didn't. He was too busy making out with Jess. He wasn't thinking about Sarah at all.

Sarah resolved never to think about him, either.

Easier said than done.

The boys were still up when she got home, still playing with their ridiculous dummy. They had him propped up in a kitchen chair, holding a hand of cards, as if he was playing a game with them. She didn't have the energy to ask questions. She just wanted to get to her room as quickly as she could, climb into bed, turn out the lights, and forget this night had ever happened.

"How was the concert?" Sam asked.

"Don't ask," Sarah said. She was trying very hard not to cry.

"Not a good show?" Sonny asked. She could hear the concern in his voice. It left her inexplicably furious. How had this happened, that she was so pathetic even her *little brother* felt sorry for her?

"Look around, Sonny," Sarah snapped. "*Nothing* is good right now! I have the biggest essay of my life due in two days and I have no idea what to write. Which means I'm never getting into Columbia or getting out of this town. Mom expects me to run this entire house by myself . . . and the boy I thought I cared about is a total creep. So, yeah. Not a great show."

The boys just stared at her. So did their ugly dummy. They kept checking it, out of the corners of their eyes, as if they were expecting it to react to her rant.

"Why are you guys acting so weird?" she said.

"No reason!" Sam insisted.

"Sorry you had a bad night," Sonny said.

Sarah shook her head. She would never understand boys. Any of them. "I'm going to bed."

She'd just turned her back on them when she heard a low, unfamiliar voice say, *"Good night."*

Sarah turned back. "Who said that?"

Sam lifted the dummy and threw his voice, terribly. *"Good night!"* he made the dummy say in a froggy voice that wasn't quite his, but also wasn't quite the voice she'd just heard.

It was weird. But she was too tired for weird. So she went upstairs and didn't think about it again. Instead, she put on her pajamas, crawled into bed, tried to think about her essay, failed.

She thought about Tyler. She thought about Tyler, kissing some other girl. She let herself cry, just a little, and finally, she fell into a deep sleep.

She didn't hear the boys whispering and giggling late into the night, until they finally fell asleep, too. She didn't hear her mother finally come home and stumble straight into bed. She didn't hear a soft clatter downstairs as Slappy leaped off the kitchen chair and made his way through the dark, still house.

There was no one to see Slappy examine Sonny's science project and make a few small, secret adjustments with Sonny's screwdriver. There was no one to see him walking stiffly down the hallway, screwdriver in hand, toward Sarah's room.

He opened the door, slowly, silently. The screwdriver glinted in the moonlight. Step by step, he drew closer to the sleeping Sarah.

She blinked once, half roused from her dream. Squinted into the darkness. Flipped on a light. "Who's there?" she whispered.

But the room was still. Nothing seemed out of the ordinary. Sleep was calling. So she turned out the light and gave herself back to it.

Which meant no one but the moon witnessed Slappy raise himself to his feet again, pad softly across the room, climb into her backpack, and zip himself into the dark.

CHAPTER 10

Halloween had officially arrived in the halls of Wardenclyffe High School. Construction paper pumpkins plastered the walls, and most of the students were in some kind of costume. There were zombies, there were witches, and there were a lot of cat ears.

As Sarah opened her locker, Principal Carter's voice boomed through the PA. "This is your creeptastic principal, hoping you all have a spooky and safe Halloween."

Sarah rooted in her backpack for her history textbook. Instead, she found Sonny's ventriloquist dummy. "What the—"

She yanked the dummy out of her bag, exasperated. It was just like Sam and Sonny to hatch some stupid prank like this. What was even the point? Did they just want to embarrass her by making sure someone at school caught her with a *doll*?

She shoved it quickly into the locker, slamming it shut just as someone leaped in front of her, shouting, "Boo!"

It was Tyler.

53

Great, she thought. This day just kept getting better and better.

"Missed you at the show last night," Tyler said. He was acting like nothing had changed.

"I bet you did," Sarah said coldly. "You have fun?"

He shrugged. "It was okay. A bunch of us were just hanging out, totally casual."

"Right." She turned her back on him, pretending to be very interested in her locker combination.

"Anyway, Mr. Harding's making me help decorate the auditorium for Halloween," Tyler said. The sound of his voice, the way he was so sure he could charm her, was making her blood boil. "Wanna ditch class and help me hang stuff?"

"Can't," she said shortly. "I have an English test."

She opened the locker, just wide enough to let her reach in and pull out her English book. But the door swung open far enough to let Tyler catch a glimpse of the doll.

"What's up with the dummy?" he asked.

"Oh, him? Nothing," Sarah said. "We're just 'hanging out.' Totally casual."

She could see from the look on his face that he understood she was mad, but had no idea why. *Good,* she decided. He didn't deserve an explanation. He didn't deserve anything from Sarah. Not anymore.

*   *   *

Tyler balanced precariously on the top rung of the ladder and pinned another tissue paper ghost to the ceiling. He couldn't believe he'd gotten suckered into decorating the auditorium. But it was better than detention.

"Fly, little ghost!" he said, giving it a spin.

He wished that Sarah had joined him, though. He couldn't figure out why she was being such a pill. He hated when girls did that, got in some kind of *mood* and then made you figure out why. It wasn't fun, and Tyler only liked things that were fun. That was supposed to be the point of girls. That was, as far as Tyler was concerned, the point of everything.

He grabbed another ghost, just as he heard the auditorium doors open and shut. Maybe Sarah had come to join him after all.

"Yo. Whoever you are, can you pass up more pins? I'm almost out," he called.

No answer.

Very carefully, so as not to lose his balance, Tyler twisted around to see who was there.

There was no one. No person, at least.

Only that creepy ventriloquist dummy from Sarah's locker, somehow standing on its own in the middle of the empty aisle.

"Okay, that's hilarious," Tyler said. "Sarah?"

She must be hiding somewhere. She'd come out when she was ready. He pinned another ghost to the ceiling, then turned back to check on the dummy.

It wasn't there anymore.

It was standing at the bottom of the ladder.

Tyler's surprise threw him off balance, just for a moment. He pinwheeled his arms, then pressed his palms flat on top of the ladder to steady himself, just in time. His heart was racing. "Not funny," he said loudly. "Sarah, stop fooling around."

The dummy's head swiveled up at the sound of his voice.

Tyler thought he must be seeing things. No way could this dummy actually be—

"I'd say you're the one fooling around," the dummy rasped.

The doll turned to stare fiercely at one of the bolts in the ladder. To Tyler's disbelief—and horror—the bolt began to turn on its own.

"What? How are you talking?" Tyler said, his voice shaking.

The bolt pulled itself out of the ladder and clattered on the ground. The doll fixed his eyes on a second bolt. It twisted . . . loosened . . . Tyler could feel the ladder buckle beneath him. "Wait, no!" he cried. "What are you doing?"

"Tell me, Tyler," the dummy said. "What's it say on that top step?"

Tyler couldn't believe he was having a conversation with a wooden dummy. But he did as he was asked and read the warning on the ladder's top step. "It says, Not a step."

The dummy grinned evilly. "Maybe you'll remember that the next time you step out of line with my sister."

With a nod of the dummy's head, the rest of the ladder's bolts went flying. All of them at once. The ladder split apart. There was a loud, clanging clash and clatter as it collapsed into a heap of useless rungs. Tyler screamed as he went down with it.

Word traveled fast. By the time the ambulance arrived, half the school had gathered on the curb to watch. Sarah stood at the front of the crowd, horrified, as they carried Tyler out of the building on a stretcher. He was strapped down, bruised and ranting.

"You have to believe me!" he shouted wildly. "It was a puppet who did this. He . . . he has *powers!* He can move things with his mind!" Then Tyler caught sight of Sarah and pointed with a shaky arm. "She knows the dummy!" he shouted. "Ask her! It was in her locker!"

He was still yelling as they loaded him into the back of the ambulance and shut the door. The sirens blared. The ambulance sped away. The crowd scattered back. Sarah didn't move. Tyler's words echoed in her ears.

She knows the dummy.

He must have hit his head when he fell. That was the only possible explanation.

Then Sarah *did* move, quickly—back to her locker, to check on the doll. Just in case. She spun the combination, pulled the door open, and gasped.

The locker was empty. The dummy was gone.

Sonny looked out at the bored faces of his middle school classmates. They had already sat through three science presentations that morning, and he could tell they were just counting the seconds for the bell to ring. They didn't realize he was about to blow their minds.

He hoped.

"Was Nikola Tesla mad?" he said. "Maybe." He flipped on the PowerPoint slide of Tesla's face. "But so are most geniuses who see the future before everybody else." He was holding his stack of note cards, but he didn't need to look down at them. He'd practiced this presentation so much, he had it memorized. "Tesla constructed this tower right here in Wardenclyffe to beam electricity across the world. Today, we're gonna beam it across this classroom."

Slouched in the back row, Tommy Madigan snickered. "Somebody beam me *out* of this classroom."

Sonny ignored him. "May I have a volunteer?"

Jenny Schmidt raised her hand and skipped to the front of the room, her perky ponytail bobbing with each step. Sonny handed her a light bulb. Then he put on his protective goggles and made a silent wish. It would work this time—it had to.

"Behold!" he boomed. "The power of Tesla . . ."

He took a deep breath and flipped the switch. Electricity crackled as the miniature Tesla tower came to sparking life. Ten feet away, the light bulb in Jenny's hand began to glow.

The class let out an astonished breath in unison. Even Tommy looked impressed. Sonny was pretty impressed himself. He'd done it! The light bulb was glowing brighter and brighter.

Actually, Sonny realized, the light bulb was getting *really* bright. Like so bright it seemed like it might—

POP!

The bulb exploded in Jenny's hand. She shrieked and leaped backward.

Their science teacher sprang into action. "Mr. Quinn, unplug the—"

ZAP!

A bolt of lightning shot out of the tower, straight at Mr. McKinley, who ducked just in time. The blast of electricity seared straight into his bookshelf instead. The dense stack of chemistry books sizzled and fried. The tower shot out another bolt, and a shelf full of beakers exploded.

After that, the room went wild. The kids scattered in terror, diving under desks and into closets as the tower began spitting lightning all over the place.

There was no escape.

CHAPTER 11

The classroom air was thick with smoke and screaming. Electric bolts seared in all directions. One of them blasted a hole in the ceiling, and plaster rained down on the class. Another blasted a giant hole in the wall. Sonny lunged for the power outlet and yanked the cord out of the wall, cutting the power.

The tower fizzled out and went dark.

The room fell silent.

Slowly, hesitantly, students began to emerge from their hiding places. A teacher's face peered through the hole in the wall. "What happened over there?" she asked, taking in the destruction.

Sonny still stood at the front of the classroom, surrounded by wreckage. He wasn't sure what he had done. Or what he was supposed to do next.

So he finished his presentation.

"And, uh, that is my report on Nikola Tesla . . . Any questions?"

As if on cue, the fire alarm started to blare. Then the sprinkler system kicked in, showering them all in cold water.

Sam looked at Sonny with pride. Jenny Schmidt, whose face was covered in black ash and whose previously shiny ponytail had morphed into a mess of frizz, looked at him with hatred. "Today is picture day!" she hissed.

Sonny didn't know what to say, but conveniently the teacher was urging everyone out of the building. Sonny could hear sirens in the distance. This was turning into a huge disaster—and he'd made it happen! He knew he should feel guilty.

But he mostly felt powerful.

"Did you see that?" Sonny gushed to Sam as they rushed toward the exit. "I finally got it to work!" He wondered if this was how Tesla felt, after his first experimental success. "I mean, maybe too much . . . but, still, I really did it!"

"Mr. Quinn!" Their science teacher was rushing toward them, looking very displeased. "We need to speak."

Sam and Sonny walked faster, trying to lose themselves in the crowd of students flowing out of the school.

"Hey, don't move another step!" Mr. McKinley called to them.

They moved several more steps, very quickly, and made it safely into the parking lot, out of Mr. McKinley's reach. From a safe distance, they watched a fire engine screech to a stop in front of the school. Firefighters piled out and surged into the building as students milled about, laughing and pointing. Everyone was excited to have a reason to leave early.

Sam was grinning from ear to ear, but Sonny was starting to realize that this might get much worse before it got

62

better. He'd escaped today—but tomorrow, he'd have to go back. And Mr. McKinley would be waiting.

"They're gonna make me repeat seventh grade," he said despairingly.

Before Sam could reassure him—or agree with him—Sarah's station wagon pulled up beside them. She rolled down the window and stared in dismay at the middle school.

A second fire engine had pulled up. The alarm was still blaring.

"Please tell me you didn't have anything to do with this," she begged her brother.

"Sonny blew up the science classroom!" Sam exclaimed. "So cool!"

"It was an accident," Sonny insisted. "What are you doing here?"

Sarah looked skeptical. "Yeah, well, there's been a couple of accidents today. Tyler Mitchell just got loaded into an ambulance. He said the dummy you guys put in my backpack attacked him with supernatural powers."

Sam tried to keep his expression perfectly blank.

"Um. We didn't put Slappy in your backpack this morning," Sonny said.

"Get in." Sarah unlocked the car doors. "And start explaining."

They tried to fill her in. By the time they finished, they were almost home.

"You discovered a walking, talking dummy and didn't

tell me?" she cried. Then she suddenly hit the brakes, a second before the car rolled over a squirrel. Sonny cringed. His sister wasn't great at yelling and driving at the same time.

"The dummy told us to keep it a secret," Sonny said. Even he knew it was a lame excuse.

"A, I'm your sister," Sarah said. "B, as a general rule, when an animated doll tells you to keep secrets, that's a red flag."

Sonny had to admit: She had a point.

"He's more than just some doll," Sam protested. "He's got powers. He can move things with his mind."

"Sonny, this is insane!" Sarah sounded like she was about to explode. Sonny knew exactly how she felt. "So why did he go after Tyler?" Sarah went on.

"Because you were complaining about Tyler after the concert last night," Sonny reminded her. "He probably just wanted to help you with your problems, just like he wanted to help me with mine . . ."

Oh, he thought, realizing that someone must have "helped" with his science presentation—and realizing who that someone must be. *Oh, no.*

"Great. What else did I complain about last night?" Sarah asked.

Sonny thought back through their conversation, horror dawning over him as he realized the answer. He met his sister's eyes in the rearview mirror, and together they exclaimed, "He's going after Mom!"

CHAPTER 12

The station wagon skidded into the driveway, and Sarah slammed on the brakes. They jumped out of the car.

"Hey, kids!" Mr. Chu called from next door. "Want to see the mummies come to life?"

"Sorry, Mr. Chu," Sarah cried.

"Can't talk right now," panted Sonny as they raced for the house and burst through the front door.

Their mother was sitting calmly on the living room couch.

And Slappy the dummy was sitting on her lap.

"Mom?" Sarah said, hesitatingly, trying not to alarm her.

Her mother was peering closely at the doll, trying to figure out how it worked. "You didn't tell me you got a ventriloquist dummy!" she said, slipping her hand up the doll's suit so she could access its controls. "How fun. He was sitting at the kitchen table like a real person."

She tugged on the lever that made Slappy's mouth move and dropped her voice very low. *"Hey, kids, my name is Bobo! And I like listening to Mom!"*

"Mom, his name is Slappy," Sonny said nervously. "And I really wouldn't do that if I were you."

"Slappy?" She laughed. "That's a ridiculous name." Their mother bent an ear toward the dummy. "What's that, Bobo?" Then she used her ventriloquism voice again, which sounded nothing like Slappy's actual voice. *"I think you work so hard and no one appreciates how giving and wonderful you are."* She shook the dummy's hand and, in her own voice, said, "Wow, Bobo, thank you for noticing."

Even in the midst of her panic, Sarah had time to think, *My whole family is so* weird.

"Mom, put him down, please!" Sonny pleaded.

"Honey, I'm just having a little fun. Relax, I won't hurt him."

"Mom, you don't understand," Sonny said.

"Mrs. Quinn, he's alive," Sam put in.

Slappy's head swiveled toward the boys and glared at them, as if in warning. Their mother didn't notice.

"I don't know about you, Bobo," she told the dummy cheerfully, "but I think these kids are trying to play a Halloween prank on us."

Before she could say anything more, the phone rang. She went off to get it—leaving the rest of them alone with the dummy.

"Hi, kids," he rasped, instantly coming back to life. *"Good day at school?"*

Sarah backed away. It was one thing to hear about a living dummy. It was another to actually *see* it. "He sounds even creepier than he looks," she whispered.

"Oh, stop. I'm blushing," said Slappy. *"So what seems to be the problem?"*

"What were you going to do to our mother?" Sonny asked suspiciously.

"Just getting to know her," Slappy said. *"Don't be jealous. I think she likes me. We're gonna be such a happy family."*

Sarah seriously didn't like the sound of that. "We're not your family, Slappy," she told him. "Do it, Sonny. Turn him off."

She was really, *really* hoping he could do it. Sonny pulled out the scrap of paper he'd found along with the dummy. He looked very worried.

Slappy, on the other hand, didn't seem worried at all. *"Hearing you say that makes me sad,"* he said, his mouth turning downward in an exaggerated frown.

For one of the first times in his life, Sonny did exactly what his sister asked him to do. He read the strange incantation carefully and loudly. *"Karru Marri Odonna Loma . . ."*

The doll's eyes slowly started to close. Some of the life drained out of his body.

". . . Molonu Karrano!"

Slappy's eyes shut. His head slumped. He was gone.

"It worked," Sam said, sounding almost sorry.

Slappy's mouth opened. *"And when I get sad . . ."* His head popped up again. His eyes opened, blazing with rage. *"I get very,* very *mad."*

"Anything you want to tell me?" Sarah's mother said, returning to the room.

The dummy went limp the moment she appeared. Sarah let out the breath she'd been holding. But this was only a temporary escape.

"Yes, Mom, we've been trying to," Sonny said, in a panicked voice. "This dummy is evil."

"You blew up the science lab!" their mother shouted. She was radiating fury.

Sonny looked like he'd almost forgotten. "Oh. There was that, too."

"That was the school calling," she said. "Do you have any idea the amount of damage you did?"

"Mom, it wasn't Sonny's fault," Sarah tried, even though she knew there was little point. Their mother was very good at not hearing things she didn't want to hear.

"I understand it was an accident," she said, "but—"

"It wasn't an accident," Sonny protested. *"He* did it!" Sonny pointed an accusing finger at Slappy.

Sarah's mother turned toward the dummy, then back to Sam, then, very slowly, said, "Excuse me? The dummy did it?"

"Yes!" all three kids exclaimed together.

For a moment, Sarah actually thought she might believe

them. Then her mother rolled her eyes. "Do *I* look like a dummy to you?"

"Mom, we're telling the truth," Sarah said.

"Truth?" Sarah's mother sounded angrier than she had in a long time. She sounded like a woman at the end of her rope. Like a woman whose son had blown up the science lab and blamed it on a wooden doll. Sarah couldn't exactly blame her.

"Here's some truth for you. Halloween is *canceled* for the three of you. Nobody leaves this house tonight. No costumes. No trick or treating. No candy. Canceled."

She threw her phone in her bag and slung it over her shoulder, because as usual, she had to go back to work. "I expect this craziness from the boys, Sarah. But I thought I could count on *you* to keep things under control."

"Mom!" Sarah couldn't believe it. Her mother was going to somehow blame all of this on *her*?

"I am so disappointed in you guys," their mother said, and slammed the door on her way out.

"Not as disappointed as I am," Slappy told them once she was gone.

This was quickly turning into an emergency. "My room," Sarah told the boys. "Now."

They raced upstairs and shut the door tightly. No dummies allowed.

"We've got a problem," Sarah said. Understatement of the century.

Sam whistled. "I've never seen your mom that mad." He sounded almost impressed.

"I'm talking about the psycho dummy on our couch. We need to get rid of him—"

There was a loud thump at the door, then another. The door flew open. Slappy stood in the doorway, his eyes wide with fury. *"Did somebody call a family meeting without* me*?"*

CHAPTER 13

Sonny thought fast. "Uh, no, we were just . . . uh . . ." Being scared out of his mind was making it very hard to think at all.

"Planning a surprise for you!" Sam said hopefully.

Slappy didn't look like he was buying it. *"Well, I've got a surprise for the three of you,"* he said nastily. *"This is my house now. And while you're under my roof, I make the rules. Rule number one, no family meetings without me."*

Sonny was frozen.

Sarah, on the other hand, was already in motion. She grabbed her softball bat from the closet. Sonny watched in amazement.

"Sorry," his sister said. "But you just got voted out of the family."

Sarah didn't hesitate. She reeled back, then swung the bat smack into Slappy, whacking him all the way across the room. He hit the far wall with a loud, angry thud, then collapsed to the floor.

"Nice swing," Sonny said in a hushed voice.

Sam looked at Sarah as if she'd just revealed a superpower.

"What do we do with him now?" Sonny asked.

"Fireplace?" Sarah suggested.

Sonny thought about it. Imagined setting the doll on fire, watching the paint melt off his face, watching his body parts burn away, one by one. He shuddered. Not even a demonic dummy deserved that kind of ending. "No, I'll have nightmares for the rest of my life," he said.

"I've got a better idea," Sarah said.

An hour later, they were in the station wagon approaching the lake on the edge of town. It was a thick, dark, stinking pond of algae and storm runoff that no one ever came near if they could help it. It smelled like sewage; it looked haunted; it was perfect.

Sarah stopped the station wagon. They all climbed out and looked nervously at the suitcase chained to the roof.

Sonny cleared his throat. "Am I the only one who feels like we're committing a crime?"

"He's a dummy," Sarah said firmly. "The only crime we're committing is littering."

Wordlessly, Sam handed her the twenty-pound dumbbell they'd brought along. She tied it to the suitcase. Then, together, they hoisted the heavy weight off the car and slung it into the lake.

Sonny watched it sink beneath the murky, muddy water. Soon, it was entirely submerged: suitcase, dumbbell, dummy, and all.

The ride home was thick with awkward silence.

"We killed a puppet," Sonny finally said. He wasn't sure whether to feel relieved or guilty.

"Trust me, we had to," his sister said. "I say we just forget it ever happened because no one will believe us anyway."

Sonny nodded, hoping he looked convinced. He didn't want his sister to know he'd been seriously scared. Or that, deep down, he still was.

But she was his sister. Even from the front seat, eyes on the road, she could tell.

"Hey, Sonny," she said, more gently than usual. "Look at me. You don't have to worry about anything, okay? It's over."

Sonny thought about that suitcase sinking into the swampy water. He thought about the dummy they'd locked inside. Of course she was right—there was no reason to worry anymore. But . . . "What if it's not? Over?"

"It is," Sarah argued. "He's dead. Locked in a suitcase. At the bottom of a lake. There is no way he's getting out—"

She was interrupted by a loud thump on the roof.

Sonny's heart stopped.

73

"Unless that dummy escaped?" Sam said in a voice full of doom.

There was another thump. The car shook. And then, with a loud crack, Slappy slammed face-first into the windshield. He stared into the car, murder in his eyes. He yowled with rage. *"Who you calling dummy, dummy?!"*

CHAPTER 14

"I told you it wasn't over!" Sonny wailed in horror.

The car swerved wildly to the right. Sarah twisted the wheel sharply in the other direction, and they swerved so far to the left they nearly ran off the road. Slappy hung on with freakish strength.

"What do you want from us?" Sarah yelled.

"I just want to be part of the family."

"Hang on tight, boys!" Sarah cried. Then she slammed her foot down on the gas. "Sorry, but we've already got enough dummies in this family."

The car lurched forward and careened wildly down the road, skidding out of control. Sarah fought the steering wheel, veering back and forth, as Slappy just laughed and laughed.

The car hit a pothole at full speed and nearly tipped over. Sonny felt his stomach leap into his throat. Slappy laughed louder. Sarah cursed and swung the wheel again to the left.

But it was too late—the car's tires lost their traction and ran off the road, and with a loud crunching of metal, the car slammed hard into a tree.

Everything went very still.

"Sonny?" Sarah said, in a shaky voice.

"I'm okay," Sonny said. Then he tested his arms and legs, making sure it was true.

"Sam?" Sarah said.

"Still in one piece," Sam said. "Which is more than I can say for the car."

There was a clanging *thud* that sounded a whole lot like the bumper dropping to the ground.

They climbed out of the car. The front end was totally busted. Sonny felt his legs trembling. His pulse was still racing. He gulped air, trying to calm himself down.

"Um, where's Slappy?" Sam asked.

They checked under the car. Up the tree. No Slappy. There was no sight of him in the woods, or on the road. Slappy was gone.

It should have been a relief. Except that Sonny was pretty sure he'd be back. And he'd be angry. Sonny groaned. "I think we just made things a thousand times worse."

The car was still drivable, barely. Sarah made her way, very slowly and carefully, through the familiar streets.

The sun had set, and Halloween had fully descended on

Wardenclyffe. All around them, children happily scooped up candy and pretended to be afraid of cardboard witches and inflatable ghosts. It was easy to enjoy a fake scare when there was nothing you were scared of for real.

Sarah thought about how she'd complained to her mother that she couldn't write her college essay because life in Wardenclyffe offered her nothing to fear.

That felt like a different lifetime.

They pulled into the driveway. A line of children were filing past the animatronic decorations in Mr. Chu's yard. All of his plastic zombies and monsters were lit up and moving jerkily back and forth. The giant spider on top of his roof wiggled its legs like it was actually alive.

Sarah shuddered. She no longer saw anything fun or funny about inanimate objects coming to life.

"Don't be scared, kids," Mr. Chu was saying. He was dressed in an elaborate Frankenstein's monster costume. "Step right up. Tonight's gonna be a real thriller!"

Sarah hoped he was wrong about that. She brought the boys inside and locked the door tightly behind them. Usually that made her feel safe. Not tonight. She couldn't shake the feeling that she was locking them all inside. Who knew what else—*who* else—was inside with them.

They gathered in her room and fired up their laptops. "Okay, we need to research every instance of demonic dummy encounters in the last fifty years," Sarah told them, already typing *demonic dummies* into the search bar.

Hundreds of articles popped up, each one more ridiculous than the next. The tabloids were full of insane stories about aliens and monsters and demonic possession, and every single one of them read like a lie.

"This is all nonsense," Sam complained after they'd spent several minutes in silence, scrolling down their screens.

"This one looks kind of real," Sonny said. "It's from 2015."

He handed his laptop to Sarah. The boys crowded around her so they could all read at once. The article was from the *Delaware Register,* which sounded like a legit paper. And Sonny was right. The story sounded real. It also sounded familiar:

"A mysterious disturbance recently took place in the town of Madison, Delaware. Neighborhoods were ravaged and the high school destroyed. An FBI spokesman said unusual weather patterns were to blame. But there are rumors of a cover-up for something far stranger— sightings of giant insects, abominable snowmen, and even a demonic ventriloquist dummy."

"No way," Sam and Sonny said together.

Sarah couldn't believe it, either. Could something like this really have happened before? If it had, how come it hadn't been front page news in every paper in the country? She kept reading:

"Creatures believed only to exist in the books by horror author R.L. Stine. Some witnesses say the creatures came alive out of the books."

Sonny started, as if something had just occurred to him. "The book," he said.

"What book?" Sarah asked.

"In the abandoned house, there was this old book with a lock on it, and we unlocked it—"

Sarah moaned. "Why would you *do* that?"

"We didn't know it would bring anything to life," Sam pointed out.

Sarah felt a glimmer of hope. If a book started all this, maybe a book could end it. "Where's the book now?"

"Tommy Madigan took it," Sam said.

Sonny had stopped listening. He was typing something furiously on his laptop.

"Sonny, I'm starting to freak out here," Sarah said.

"If the books come to life, then we have to know which book it was." Sonny read aloud from the database he'd pulled up. *"From 1979 to 1985, legendary horror author R.L. Stine lived in Wardenclyffe, New York, where he started his writing career with an unpublished novel titled* Slappy Halloween, *a tale of a demonic dummy who sets out to create a family of his own by . . ."* Sam's voice trailed off. He looked up at his sister, eyes pooling with terror.

"By what?" Sarah shrieked.

"By bringing Halloween to life."

Sarah allowed herself to imagine it: Every Halloween monster in town, every witch and ghost and zombie and vampire, somehow magically made real. A waking nightmare, in her own backyard.

"Why couldn't he bring Christmas to life? Or Thanksgiving? Or National Puppy Day? Thousands of adorable puppies licking your face!" Sam exclaimed. "We need to call the cops!"

"And tell them what?" Sarah said. "That an evil dummy is about to bring Halloween to life? Great idea, Sam. They'll come and arrest us." All the hope she'd felt a moment ago had drained away. A demonic dummy was on a mission to destroy everything and everyone she cared about, and there was no one to ask for help. No one even knew about it but two thirteen-year-old boys and one Sarah Quinn.

Okay, she thought. If they were the only hope this town had, then they had no choice. They would have to stop the dummy.

"Wait!" Sonny said suddenly. "I found a number."

"For Stine?" asked Sarah in surprise.

Sonny shook his head. "No. Apparently no one knows where he is. The number's for someone named Richard Shivers, the president of the R.L. Stine Appreciation Society." He shrugged. "It's worth a try. Maybe he can tell us what to do."

Sam grabbed Sarah's cell phone and began dialing. Sarah snatched the phone away from him just in time to hear it ringing on the other end.

A pre-recorded voicemail message kicked in. *"Good day. You've reached Dr. Richard Shivers and the R.L. Stine Appreciation*

Society. If you're trying to reach Stine, don't bother. Otherwise, leave a message."

There was a loud beep. Sarah took a deep breath and began. "Hi, Dr. Shivers. My name is Sarah Quinn and I desperately need to get in touch with R.L. Stine. We're in Wardenclyffe, New York. And this is going to sound crazy, but . . . I think one of his early stories has come to life . . . Anyway, please call me back at this number. Thank you!"

Sarah hung up the phone and rose to her feet. "Looks like we're on our own. Grab your coats."

"Where are we going?"

"We need to find Tommy Madigan," she said, already on her way out the door. "We need to get that book back. Now."

On a dark, empty road on the other side of town, Slappy the dummy found what he was looking for. The small split-level house was lit up for Halloween, its stoop crowded with jack-o'-lanterns and its lawn dominated by a large, plastic Headless Horseman.

Slappy closed his eyes. He opened his wooden arms wide. Then he recited the necessary words. *"Karru Marri Odonna Loma Molonu Karrano . . ."*

The Headless Horseman lurched to life, swinging blindly from side to side and then galloping into the night. The jack-o'-lanterns blinked their pulpy eyes awake, bared orange fangs, and then sprouted wings and lifted into the sky. A skull hanging from the porch twisted toward Slappy. Its jaw-bone creaked as it gave Slappy a bony grin.

Slappy grinned back. "Slappy Halloween!"

This Halloween was, for Slappy, going to be very happy. He hummed merrily as he walked down the street, awakening each decoration he passed. By the time he reached the floodlit parking lot of a Walgreens, the night had come alive with monsters. Slappy heard screams in the distance. His smile grew.

The store was dark and quiet, manned by a single employee. His name tag read WALTER. Slappy slipped past him easily and went straight for the Halloween aisle. He found exactly what he was looking for: a collection of Goosebumps costumes.

The Abominable Snowman. The Werewolf of Fever Swamp. The Haunted Mask. Slappy pointed at each in turn, as if saying hello to old friends.

"If those kids don't want me in their family, I'll raise one of my own," he told his fellow monsters.

Then, with a single incantation, he brought every nightmare to life.

CHAPTER 15

The store was alive with monsters. But Slappy needed one more thing. And this *Walter* was just the man to supply it.

Slappy had hidden from the man behind the register with ease. Now he showed himself—flanked by his army of ghouls and monsters.

Walter's polite smile froze into a grimace of fear. "Welcome to Walgreens?"

Slappy gave him a choice. "Trick, or treat?"

The man was obviously scared out of his mind. Good.

"Uhhh, treat?"

"Wrong answer," Slappy said. "Trick."

With perfect aim, he threw an ogre mask. It landed on Walter's face and latched on tight. Walter's fingers flew to the mask, trying in desperation to peel it off and free himself.

This was futile. But Slappy enjoyed watching him try.

Slowly but surely, the mask took effect, transforming Walter, limb by limb, into a hunchbacked ogre.

"Welcome to the family," Slappy told him.

"Serving families is what I do," Walter recited in a creepy voice.

Slappy led his army of monsters into the night. He sent the witches flying off on broomsticks, the zombies lumbering toward the clumps of trick-or-treating children. But Walter the ogre, he kept by his side.

Wardenclyffe Tower loomed in the distance, silhouetted in the moonlight. Calling to him with possibility.

"Come along, brother," Slappy told his new pet ogre. "Time to turn things up a notch."

Sam and Sonny knew where Tommy lived. But this was Halloween night. No chance he was going to be sitting around at home, twiddling his thumbs. One hundred percent chance he was out somewhere in the dark, causing trouble.

Fortunately, Sonny and Sam knew exactly where that somewhere was most likely to be. Because Tommy had told them himself.

They found the goon squad right where they'd expected, tossing rolls of toilet paper into the trees on Principal Harrison's lawn. Tommy was wrapping an entire roll around one thick trunk.

"Tommy!" Sonny shouted, running toward him, Sam and Sarah hot on his heels. Definitely the first time anyone had been this happy to set eyes on Tommy Madigan.

"Tommy, we need that book!" Sonny yelled, the moment he was in earshot. "Where is it?"

"It's really important," Sam added.

"What book?" Tommy looked more clueless than usual.

"The one you took from us," Sonny said.

"Oh." Understanding dawned. "I've got that right here."

"Really?" Sonny said, not quite believing it could be this easy.

"No, idiot." Tommy laughed. A beat later, his goons clued in and laughed with him. "Why would I be carrying a book around with me on Halloween? Why don't you go home with your babysitter now—we'll be there in a little bit to egg your house."

Sonny's hands curled into fists, then released. It's not like throwing a punch would do any good. For that matter, it's not like he even knew *how* to throw a punch. Tommy mounted his bike. This was it, Sonny thought. Their only hope, riding away into the TP'd sunset.

Then Sarah yanked Tommy off the bike by his collar.

Sonny gaped. This night was showing him a whole new side of his big sister. An *awesome* side.

"Listen, you little punk," she snarled. "I'm not the baby-sitter. I'm Sonny's sister. You give us that book or I *will* make your life a living nightmare, and when I'm done with you, the only thing you'll be using that toilet paper for is to—"

"Okay!" Tommy yelped, in a voice two octaves higher

than normal. "You don't have to be so mean about it. The book's at my house. In my room."

Sarah let go, and Tommy scrambled, crab-like, out of her reach. It was only when he was a safe distance away and up on his bike that he dared add, "But it's hidden, so good luck finding it, losers!"

He and his goons rode off in one direction. Sonny led the others in the opposite direction, straight for Tommy's house. But they didn't get very far before they heard a scream.

Tommy's scream.

They turned around slowly, in time to see three witches on broomsticks yank Tommy and his friends off the ground and rocket them into the sky. Up, up, impossibly high up—and then, Tommy's screams faded into the night—*away*.

Nikola Tesla's lab was exactly how he had left it, more than one hundred years before. The equipment was a little dusty, a little old-fashioned, but it would serve Slappy's purposes just fine.

One wall was almost entirely covered by large metal levers and switches. Slappy used his psychic powers to switch them all on.

"Why settle for a small family?" he asked Walter. Walter stared back at him with a glazed, mindless look, waiting for

his next order. "Why settle, when we can project my power *everywhere*, and bring the whole town to life?"

There was a deafening grinding noise as the complex woke up for the first time in over a century. Turbines whirled. Pistons pumped. Electric current flowed through thick, twisted wires—and straight into the tower that loomed over the entire town.

All across Wardenclyffe, people dropped what they were doing and gazed at the sky. Small children dressed as scarecrows and superheroes. Kind grandparents holding out buckets of candy. Harried parents towing their kids from house to house. Teens tossing eggs and TP'ing teachers' houses.

All of them stopped cold in their tracks and watched in terrified awe as the tower glowed, spitting out bolts of lightning, like spider legs sparking across the sky.

"Karru Marri Odonna," Slappy whispered, and his voice rode the current, up the tower, straight into the sky and into every home, every lawn, every store, every nook and cranny in all of Wardenclyffe.

"Loma Molonu Karrano." The sparking tower brought his spell to the garden gnomes on Ashley Lane, the lurching Frankenstein on the middle school steps, the fanged vampires painted on a child's candy bag. And even from miles away, deep inside the laboratory complex, Slappy could hear the sweet music of screams.

Wardenclyffe had always been such a sleepy little town. Slappy cackled with glee. *Time to wake up.*

Sarah and the boys didn't notice the lightning streaking across the sky. They were too intent on their mission. Tommy's house was gray, squat, and a little sad. It was the only house on the street with no decorations.

"You sure this is Tommy's house?" Sarah asked.

"Yeah, I think he lives with his grandmother," Sonny said, and rang the bell.

No answer. They crept around to the back garden and peeked in a window. An old woman, who must have been Tommy's grandmother, was sleeping on the couch. The TV was blaring loud enough that they could hear it through the window. Nonetheless, Sarah banged hard on the glass. The woman didn't stir.

Under normal circumstances, this would be when they gave up and went home, came back another day. But there was a psychotic talking dummy out there trying to weasel his way into her family: There was nothing normal about these circumstances.

Sarah gave the window a gentle push, and it rose. "You guys climb in," she told Sonny and Sam. "Go find the book."

She gave each of them a boost to get inside. She heard a mournful howl echo in the distance.

A dog, she told herself. *Just a harmless dog. Definitely not, like, a werewolf. Probably not. Hopefully not.*

"What are you gonna do?" Sonny whispered from the window.

What *was* she going to do? Protect her family, somehow. Any way she could. There was a shovel stuck in the nearby flower bed. Sarah grabbed it and hoisted it like a bat. "Make sure nothing surprises us. Go!"

Sarah paced in circles around the house, gripping the shovel tightly. The house across the street was decorated for the holiday: two skeletons dressed as a bride and groom. She felt like they were watching her, tracking her movements through the dark. Sarah backed against the house, pressed herself to the cool stucco, prayed for the boys to hurry.

A shadow lurched down the deserted street. Sarah stiffened. She could feel her heart thumping in her chest. The figure turned its face to the full moon. The moonlight illuminated its decaying features, its peeling skin.

Zombie, Sarah whispered to herself, her mouth dry, her throat closing in terror. Not possible. Still, it was getting closer. Every muscle in her body wanted to flee. But she couldn't leave her brother behind. She had no choice. She had to stand. She had to fight.

Sarah hoisted the shovel and ducked behind a cluster of bushes. She prepared herself, letting the zombie close in. Closer, closer still, as if it could sense her . . . or could smell her delicious, tasty brains. Which it wanted to eat.

Sarah chased the thought out of her head. She focused on her brother, whom she had to protect. She focused on the shovel, heavy and sharp and ready. The zombie limped closer, about to pass right by her.

Now! Sarah thought. And with all the courage she could muster, she leaped out of the bushes with a blood-curdling scream and swung the shovel as hard as she could.

SONNY AND HIS FRIEND SAM GOT A JOB HAULING JUNK OUT OF AN ABANDONED HOUSE IN TOWN.

IT WAS PRETTY CREEPY IN THERE.

THEY FOUND A HIDDEN WOODEN CRATE WITH AN OLD, LOCKED BOOK INSIDE.

SUDDENLY, THERE WAS A VENTRILOQUIST DUMMY IN THE CRATE, LABELED SLAPPY

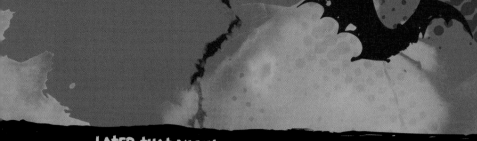

LATER THAT NIGHT, BACK AT SONNY'S HOUSE,
THEY REALIZED SLAPPY HAD COME TO LIFE!

HE TOLD THEM TO KEEP IT A SECRET.

SONNY'S SISTER, SARAH, FOUND SLAPPY IN HER BACKPACK AT SCHOOL THE NEXT DAY, AND PUT HIM IN HER LOCKER.

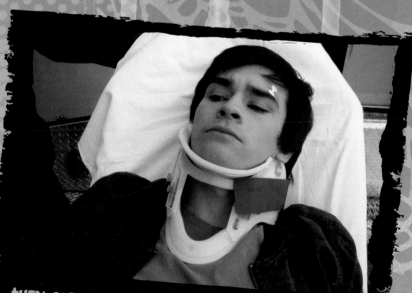

THEN SARAH'S FRIEND TYLER HAD A BAD FALL, AND HAD TO GO TO THE ER. HE BLAMED IT ON SLAPPY.

SARAH DIDN'T BELIEVE HIM—SLAPPY
WAS JUST A DOLL. BUT WHEN SHE
CHECKED HER LOCKER, HE WAS GONE!

SLAPPY HAD MAGIC POWERS AND A MIND
OF HIS OWN . . . AND HE WAS EVIL.

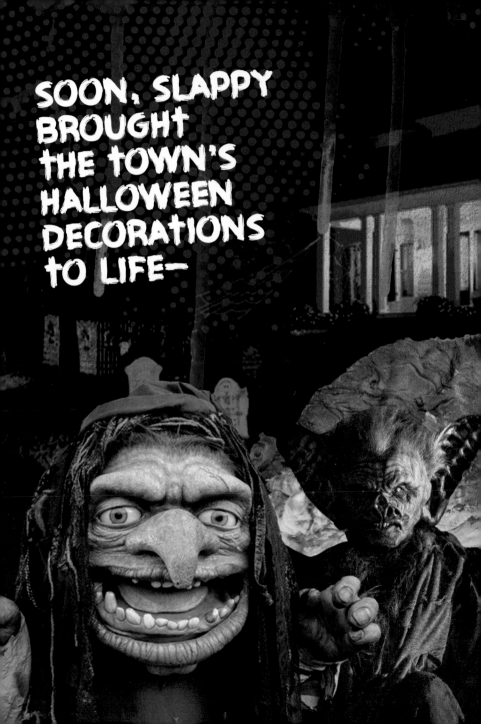

SOON, SLAPPY BROUGHT THE TOWN'S HALLOWEEN DECORATIONS TO LIFE—

SONNY REALIZED THAT THE BOOK THEY'D FOUND ALSO HAD MAGIC POWERS.

WOULD THE KIDS BE ABLE TO GET RID OF THE MONSTERS AND STOP SLAPPY'S EVIL PLANS?

CHAPTER 16

"Dude, don't hit me!" the zombie shouted, dodging out of the shovel's path just in time.

Sarah was about to take a second swing, determined not to miss this time. But she paused—the voice was oddly familiar.

"Tyler?" Sarah asked.

The zombie, crouched low with one arm wrapped protectively around his face, looked up. "Sarah?"

It was Tyler all right, wearing a sling around his arm and a cheap Halloween mask on his face. "What are you doing here?" she asked. "I thought you were in the hospital."

"I got out," Tyler said, climbing awkwardly to his feet. He looked nervously at the shovel in her hand. "It was just a mild concussion and a broken arm. What are *you* doing here?"

"Waiting for my brother," Sarah said. Behind her, the house was utterly silent, as if it had swallowed the boys whole.

"You should ditch your lame brother and come to the party with me," Tyler said. "It's over at Jess's house."

At the sound of that name—at the *nerve* of him speaking that name straight to Sarah's face—her fingers tightened on the shovel. "Oh, really?" she said coolly. "Concert Make Out Jess?"

Even behind the zombie mask, she could tell Tyler flinched. "What do you mean?"

"I was there," she told him. It felt good to finally let it out. "I saw you. The *real* you. Not cute, charming, 'I brought you a care package' you. But lying, cheating, making out with random girls you. And it took me until now to realize that I deserve so much better."

She felt like the words had been boiling inside her since that moment at the concert, and now, finally, she'd pulled off the lid, unleashed the pressure, let herself explode.

She'd thought it would hurt, letting herself finally *feel* all that rage and sorrow she'd bottled up—but this was the opposite of pain. This was a blast of joy, finally getting to tell him exactly who he was, and exactly how little she needed him.

And left behind in its wake: Calm. Certainty. The simple fact that she deserved better than him, and this was the first step toward getting it.

"So . . . I feel like I'm getting mixed signals here?" Tyler said. In addition to being lying, cheating scum, he wasn't exactly the sharpest pencil in the box. "Is that a yes or a no for the Halloween party?"

Sarah gave him an exaggerated wave farewell and tried

to put it in words even his simple brain could understand. "Bye, Tyler! You like care packages? Here's one for you: Have a nice life. I'm sticking with my brother."

Speaking of Sonny . . . What was taking him so long?

The house had three bedrooms, but only one of them had a skull and crossbones on the door, with a handwritten sign reading, *No Losers. Keep Out!*

"Looks like Tommy to me," Sonny said.

Sam, his mouth stuffed full of the gummy bears he'd stolen from the house's candy dish, said only, "Mmmf, mmm, phmmm, mmpf!"

Sonny took that as agreement and stepped inside. The room was a mess, piled high with sweaty socks and old pizza boxes, skates and basketball jerseys and comic books, all of it reeking of onions and feet, Tommy's signature smell. Sam rummaged through the closet. Sonny rooted around in the dark crawl space beneath the mattress, pulling out Tommy's treasures one by one: Box of fireworks. Moldy pizza crust. Stuffed elephant. Sonny felt like an archaeologist of garbage.

His fingers grazed the edge of something hard and leathery, something that felt like . . . could it be . . . ?

He stretched as far as he could, managed to get hold of the object, yanked it out, and let out a cry of triumph. "Found it!"

This was it, the leather manuscript they'd recovered from

the abandoned old house—and on its cover was an inscription Sonny hadn't noticed before: *R.L. Stine.*

Until that moment, he hadn't quite believed it was possible: that monsters could climb out of books. He hugged it to his chest. Somewhere in these pages, there would be a solution. There had to be.

The lights flickered.

"Uh, what was that?" Sam asked.

Sonny didn't want to stick around and find out. "Let's go."

Before they left, though, Sam insisted on making another detour to the candy bowl brimming with gummy bears. It was guarded by a waxen, disembodied hand, the sole Halloween decoration in the house.

"Some for the road," Sam said, scooping one fistful into his mouth and reaching back into the bowl to grab another for later.

The hand grabbed back.

"Ahhhh!" Sam shrieked and tried to pull his arm away, but the disembodied hand held on tight.

"What are you doing?!" Sonny whisper-shouted.

"It . . . it has my hand!" Sam cried.

Sonny watched helplessly as Sam whirled the hand through the air, whacked it against the table, the wall, anything to get it to let go. Finally, he managed to fling the hand across the room, a fleet of gummy bears sailing along with it.

Sam crumpled to the floor in relief, then started at the sound of a giggle.

Sonny checked out Tommy's grandmother: still sleeping on the couch.

There was a second giggle, louder this time.

Sonny squinted into the darkness of the living room and drew in a sharp breath. "Sam," he said, in a hushed voice. "Turn around . . . *very slowly.*"

Sam turned around. Sonny pointed to the carpet—where a regiment of gummy bears was marching toward their feet.

Sam crouched, gleeful. "Aww, they're just gummy bears!" He reached out to poke one of them in its soft candy belly. "Hey there, little guys."

"You just *ate* all their brothers and sisters," Sonny warned them. "I wouldn't—"

Sam squeaked and jumped backward as the little gummy bears melted into one another, transforming themselves into much, much bigger bears.

"Maybe they want us to stay and play?" Sam said hopefully.

The bears didn't look like they wanted a game. They looked more like they wanted a war.

One of the bears grabbed a porcelain teapot from a dusty shelf and flung it at Sam's head.

The battle was on.

95

Cups and dishes flew through the air. Gummy bears bounced off the floor and ceiling. Sam and Sonny weaved and dodged. Ducked and covered. As the bears closed in, they plunged fists into gummy stomachs and gummy heads, to no avail. The bears always bounced back. They bounced and flung and kicked and *would not stop* giggling.

The giggling is the worst, Sonny thought as he ducked behind a china cabinet. A ceramic clown crashed into the wall just over his head, followed by a ceramic tiger, a ceramic ballet dancer, and a ceramic cat.

Tommy's grandmother snored through the whole thing.

"Sam, I need some help over here!" Sonny cried. But Sam was in no condition to help him. The gummy bears had him by the ankles and were dragging him toward the kitchen. Sonny imagined an entire cupboard filled with gummy bears: *reinforcements.*

His phone vibrated and, without thinking, he picked it up.

"Sonny?" It was his mom.

"Mom? Help! We're under attack!"

"What are you talking about?" she asked, sounding very small and very far away. "Where's Sarah? Who's attacking you?"

"Gummy bears!" Sonny said, realizing how ridiculous that sounded. Before he could say anything else, a giant gummy bear dropped from the chandelier and plopped on his head. It oozed down his body, completely encasing him in gummy.

Sonny heard his mom say, "That's it—I'm coming home!" as he dropped the phone to try to fight the gummy. He summoned all his strength. Then he plunged his fists straight into gummy hide and yanked as hard as he could. He flung the bear off of him and took a gasping breath of gummy-free air.

His relief lasted only seconds. The bear bounced off the far wall and lunged back toward Sonny, scooping up a pair of knitting needles from the coffee table. The bear wielded the needles like two swords, both aimed straight at Sonny's face.

Sonny grabbed the heavy, leather-bound book and held it in front of him in desperation. The needles bounced off its stiff cover.

The bear changed its strategy and started stabbing Sonny's fingers one by one, trying to get him to drop the book. Drops of blood spattered the floor. His grip on the book loosened. The cover fell open and—

WHOOOOOSH!

An enormous wind sucked the gummy bear off its feet and into the book. With a loud sucking sound and a sharp pop, the gummy bear flattened against the page—and disappeared.

CHAPTER 17

Sonny looked at the manuscript in amazement. He realized: It wasn't just a book, it was a *weapon*.

"Sam, I'm coming!" Sonny yelled, running toward the kitchen.

He stopped short in the doorway. The gummy bears attacking Sam had melted into one another again—all of them. The result was one towering gummy bear, at least seven feet tall. It loomed over Sam, giggling in a low, rumbling voice. The bear backed Sam into a corner and raised its gummy foot, preparing to stomp.

Sonny aimed the book. *This better work*, he thought. Then he opened the cover.

WHOOOOOOOSH!

The book's powerful wind swirled around the giant bear, which dissolved into hundreds of tiny gummy bears. Trapped in the whirlwind, they whipped and circled through the air, drawn inexorably toward the book.

One by one, they disappeared. Sonny slammed the cover shut.

Sam shook himself off, looking surprised to discover he was still in one piece. "Best book ever," he said.

He and Sonny both startled at the sound of a loud bang on the window—what now?

But it was only Sarah, gesturing wildly for them to climb out.

Sonny pushed the window open and scrambled out of the house. His hands were sticky. He could still taste sugar on his tongue.

It's going to be a long time before I eat another gummy bear, he thought.

"What were you doing in there?" Sarah asked, sounding irritated.

"Oh, no big deal," Sam said. "Just being mauled by our favorite comfort food."

"Sarah, everything's *alive,*" Sonny told his sister. "I mean, even candy!"

Sarah didn't seem concerned. She'd caught sight of the book. "Is that the book? Let's read it."

"There's something you should know about this book," Sonny said. He wasn't quite ready to let it out of his hands yet.

"What?"

Before he could answer, a skeleton dressed like a bride charged out of the bushes—and straight toward Sarah.

Sam screamed. Sonny ducked. Sarah stood her ground, raised her shovel, and conked the skeleton on the head. The bones scattered in a heap of lace and satin.

"Sarah, behind you!" Sonny shouted, as a groom skeleton jerked the shovel out of her hand. The skeleton raised the shovel over his head, ready to strike.

Sonny opened the book and thrust it toward the skeleton. A *whooooosh*, a powerful burst of wind, and both skeletons were sucked neatly into the book.

Sonny slammed it shut and hugged it tight. "That's what," he told his sister, who was still gaping in confusion at the ground where the bride skeleton had fallen. There was nothing of it left but its bouquet of dead roses, each with a blinking eyeball dead center. "This is no normal book."

They had to find somewhere safe. Sarah led them through the dark suburban streets and into a narrow alleyway behind two sets of houses, then stopped.

"Uh, why are we stopping in the creepiest alley in Wardenclyffe?" Sonny asked, confused. "Tonight of all nights?"

"Because nobody decorates an alley for Halloween," Sarah pointed out. "We need to read the book and see how we can end this."

Sam grabbed the book out of Sonny's hands. "I got this." He flipped the book open and started reading in his best British accent. (Which was terrible.) *"It was a dark and stormy night. The damp air dripped with terror—"*

Sarah lost patience after about thirty seconds and snatched the book out of Sam's hands. She thumbed quickly through the pages, murmuring as she scanned the text. *"Slappy was a lonely dummy who wanted a family of his own—*check. *His revenge was to create a family by bringing Halloween to life—*check. *But that wasn't enough—"*

"Why not?" Sam said. "Seems like plenty of revenge to me."

"Because Slappy wanted more than just a family," Sarah read. *"He wanted a mother. So his plan was to—"* She stopped abruptly. Her chin was trembling.

"Was to what?" Sonny said, impatient. "Keep reading!"

"I can't!" Sarah said. "That was the last page. It's an unfinished manuscript." She held up the book to show them: The final pages were blank. Her hand was trembling, too, Sonny noticed.

Slappy wanted a mother, Sonny thought. A terrible idea struck him.

Slappy knew exactly where to get one.

"Well, *now* what do we do?" he said.

Sarah said what they were all thinking. "Slappy's going to go after Mom." Her voice sounded flat and determined. Dead. "This book is the only thing that can stop him. We have to get to the nursing home and save her."

"Mom's not at the nursing home," Sonny admitted, stomach sinking. He'd somehow managed to make everything worse.

"Where is she?" Sarah asked.

"On her way home to save us."

"What?" Sarah looked like she wanted to strangle him.

"She called while we were getting attacked by gummy bears!"

"Why would you answer the phone at a time like that?" Sarah asked.

"I don't know! Maybe because unlike you, I actually take Mom's calls."

"Wow, really?" Sarah glared at him. "Guilt trip much? If you weren't always messing everything up around the house—"

"Hey, guys?" Sam waved his arms to get their attention. Sonny had almost forgotten his best friend was there. "I realize we're tapping into some deep-rooted sibling issues here, but we need to find your mom . . . before Slappy does!"

Kathy Quinn could tell from the panicked sound of her son's voice over the phone that something was seriously wrong. She walked out of work in the middle of her shift and drove toward home as quickly as she could.

Sarah was a responsible teenager, Kathy knew that. But she was still a teenager. And this was Halloween. Who knew what kind of trouble they might all be getting into?

The streets were full of trick-or-treaters. She spotted one dressed as an inflatable ghoul, dragging a very real-looking power cord, and another dressed as the Headless Horseman—riding a very real horse!

Kathy shook her head in wonder. She couldn't imagine having the time, much less the energy, to put so much effort into a costume. It did look like fun, though, pretending to be terrified. The two kids running away from a walking jack-o'-lantern were doing an especially good job of acting scared out of their minds.

As she turned onto her block, she passed an abandoned police car, its doors open, its sirens still blaring. The sidewalks and street were crowded with her neighbors, all running panicked in the same direction—away from her house.

"Oh, no," Kathy said aloud. "What did those boys do?"

She wove carefully through the scattering pedestrians and pulled into her driveway, nearly hitting some jerk in a werewolf costume who flung himself in front of the car. Kathy hit the brakes just in time. "Watch it, pal!" she shouted out the window. These trick-or-treaters were out of control.

She got out of the car, ready to give the werewolf a piece of her mind—or at least some stern advice about safe pedestrian behavior—but he loped away too quickly.

Kathy hurried toward the house. She had her own reckless kids to worry about. But something stopped her in her tracks—the strange, insistent sensation that someone was watching her.

Kathy looked behind her: nothing. The trick-or-treaters had all fled. The street, the yards, the whole block was deserted.

There was a strange rustling sound from the branches above. Out of the corner of her eye, Kathy caught a flicker of movement.

There was something sinister about it. Something not quite human. She looked up, to see eight giant black eyes blinking back at her. Eight impossibly long legs stretched out through the branches. They seemed to be made of . . . *balloons*?

Kathy rubbed her eyes, sure she was imagining things. But she wasn't imagining the long, silvery strand of web that unspooled from the gigantic spider's belly. She wasn't imagining it wrapping her tight in its sticky grasp.

There was no one to notice as the spider tugged Kathy's wriggling, trapped body off the ground and into its web.

There was no one to hear her scream.

CHAPTER 10

Their block looked like a war zone, and it was easy to see why. Mr. Chu's balloon spider had come to life. It had woven an enormous web stretching from roof to roof and tree to tree. Familiar faces peeked out of silvery cocoons, all of them dangling from the web, trapped and waiting for the spider to come back—and feed.

Sarah noticed her brother's face had gone paper white. He *hated* spiders.

Their mother's car was in the driveway, its door open.

She never left the car door open.

"Where's Mom?" Sarah cried.

"There!" Sonny shouted, pointing up at the tree.

Sarah gasped. Her mother was cocooned like the others, dangling at least twenty feet up, in a tree in Mr. Chu's front yard. She looked helplessly down at her kids, lips moving, but Sarah couldn't make out what she as saying. They had to get her down, *now*.

The spider had scrambled down Mr. Chu's roof and into his backyard, but who knew how long before it was back.

"Now's our chance," she said. "Sonny, give me the book. You guys go get our ladder. Meet me at the tree!"

She raced toward the tree where her mother hung, dodging and zigzagging past the assortment of ghouls, goblins, and mummies roaming across the neighborhood. She recognized all of them as decorations from Mr. Chu's yard, and shook her head. Of all the years to go *big*.

She nearly ran smack into a mummy, but flipped the book open just in time. The monster was sucked inside, leaving behind only a single, ratty bandage. It floated onto the grass.

"Wait a second," Sarah said. "Why am *I* running away from *them*?" After all, she had the ultimate weapon. Maybe it was time to use it.

Sonny and Sam ran for the house. There was a ladder under the front staircase that should be tall enough to rescue his mother. Just one problem: The staircase was inside the house. And to get inside the house, he and Sam would have to make it past the battle line of jack-o'-lanterns assembled on the porch.

Their leader, Sam's soldier pumpkin, the army hat still propped on its head, ordered them to halt.

Sonny recognized one of the pumpkins he'd carved, its mouth carefully molded into a rictus of rage. "Where do you think you're going?" it growled. Its eyes were made of fire.

"No way . . ." Sam breathed.

"Uh, we need to get in our house?" Sonny said. He wondered: If he had created this pumpkin, did that mean he controlled it?

The pumpkin inhaled deeply, then blew a jet of fire at the boys. They backed away hastily. Sonny felt the sharp heat singe his eyebrows.

So much for control.

"Not on my watch, soldier," said Sam's pumpkin sergeant.

"I told you we should have just kept it simple!" Sam complained. "But no, we had to let the pumpkin 'guide' us. We carved monsters, Sonny!"

Sonny's pumpkin laughed with diabolical glee. "That's right. And look what you did to poor Terry." The jack-o'-lantern rolled its fiery eyes toward a misshapen pumpkin at the end of the porch. It was Sam's first try, the one with the collapsed face full of pulp.

"Hiya!" Terry boomed, sounding more goofy than goosebump-y.

Sonny felt kind of sorry for him. Even though he was pretty sure this deformed fool of a pumpkin wanted him dead as much as all the others.

"Sorry, dude," Sam said.

"You're about to be *real* sorry," the angry one warned. "Sergeant Squash, open fire!"

The soldier pumpkin opened its jaw and unleashed a barrage of pumpkin seeds, forcing Sonny to the ground. "Ow! That stings!" he cried.

Meanwhile, Sonny's pumpkin unleashed another flame attack. Sonny crawled toward a nearby trash can lid and grabbed it, using it to shield himself from the heat. Sam cowered behind it with him.

"Stomp on him!" Sonny shouted. Together, shielded by the lid, they charged the pumpkins. Sam slammed a foot down through Sergeant Squash's squishy head.

"I'm hit!" the army pumpkin cried. "Medic!"

Sam yanked the flame-shooting pumpkin off the porch and smashed it into poor Terry. The pumpkins exploded into each other with a disgusting, pulpy, orange *SPLAT.*

"Boom," Sam crowed. "You just got squashed."

Sarah had battled her way through enough monsters to reach the trunk of her mother's tree. Kathy was wrapped so tightly in the spider's cocoon that she could only move her head, but she craned her neck as far as she could to catch sight of her daughter.

"Honey, I was so worried!" she called down. "Are you all right?"

"I'm fine," Sarah assured her mother. "Just hang tight." As if she had any other choice.

"I should have trusted you," her mother admitted. "I thought you guys were making up all that stuff about the dummy, but— Look out behind you!"

Sarah whirled around. A mummy reached for her, its

bandaged hands inches from her throat. She ducked beneath its grasp and opened the book. *WHOOOOOSH.*

"Sarah, go right!" her mother shouted. She had a perfect bird's-eye view of the monsters closing in on Sarah from all sides. "I mean, left! I mean, your right, my left!"

Sarah danced from mummy to mummy, sucking them into the book one by one, and she didn't have time to listen to her mother's confused advice. "Really, Mom? You're micromanaging right now?" she shouted, vanquishing yet another one. "Mom, I got this. We're gonna get you down, I promise. You just need to trust me."

She locked eyes with her mother, willing her, for just this once, to see that she was strong and competent and could handle the world on her own.

Her mother smiled proudly. "I love you, Sarah. And— Ghost! Three o'clock!"

Sarah spun around, already wielding the book, but before she could take aim, the ghost knocked it right out of her hand. The heavy manuscript sailed across the lawn and landed with a thump. Sarah lunged for it, but another ghost swooped in and clamped down on it with its wide white mouth, and then flew away.

"No!" Sarah screamed, chasing after the ghost. It was nothing but a white bedsheet with eyeholes—and it was getting away. She leaped as high as she could and grabbed a fistful of sheet. For a second, she thought she had it . . .

Until the ghost lifted her off of her feet and into the sky.

Sarah hung on tight, as determined as she was frightened. She could not let the book get away.

They sailed past Sonny and up toward her mother's tree branch.

"Sarah, let go of that ghost!" her mother shouted.

"Sarah, *do not* let go of that ghost!" Sonny yelled at the same time.

The ghost veered sharply to the right, Sarah hung on as best she could, but her hands were sweaty, her grip slick. The bedsheet was slipping from her grasp. Her arms felt like they were tearing out of their sockets. *Hang on*, she told herself. *Hang. On.*

But it was no use. The ghost whipped around to the left, flinging Sarah with enough force that her grip gave way. She plummeted to the lawn and landed with a teeth-rattling thud.

"Are you okay?" Sonny asked, rushing over.

"I'm fine!" Sarah groaned, hoping it was true. Everything hurt; she felt like one giant bruise. "Get Mom!"

As if it heard her and knew its dinner was about to get away, the giant balloon spider crested over Mr. Chu's roof with a hideous shriek. It extended one of its balloon legs toward Mrs. Quinn, and another straight at Sarah, who was still dusting herself off and testing out each of her limbs.

Sam grabbed a lawn stake and popped as many balloons as he could. But each *pop* unleashed an army of real spiders. They swarmed. Sarah, Sonny, and Sam screamed in unison,

desperately brushing off the endless spider march—while two black balloon legs lifted their mother into the sky and carried her away.

As soon as their spider queen was gone, the little spiders skittered off into the darkness, but it was too late. Their mother was gone. The book was gone. They had no more weapon, no more plan, no more hope.

The three kids sank to the ground. For the first time that night, they realized that the sky was wild with lightning, all of it spurting from Tesla's distant tower.

"Slappy brought the tower to life," Sonny said, impressed in spite of himself. "That's how this is happening."

"We have to stop him," Sarah said, which was stating the obvious. The question was how.

"Uhhh . . . guys?" said Sam.

There was another, more pressing question, and that was how they would escape from a yard full of Halloween monsters when they no longer had the book. They looked at one another, and then at the mummies, zombies, ghosts, and vampires closing in on them from all sides.

Wordlessly, they backed toward Mr. Chu's front door, their only path of possible escape.

Or so they thought . . . until a giant mummy emerged from the depths of the house, wrapped all three of them in its powerful arms, and yanked them inside.

CHAPTER 19

The mummy dumped them on the tile floor, hard. Then he unwound the bandages covering his face.

"It's me!" he said. "Mr. Chu!"

Sonny blinked. "Mr. Chu?" He'd never been so happy to see his neighbor. Though it was hard not to hold a grudge about the gigantic, mom-kidnapping, balloon spider.

"Shhh!" Mr. Chu bolted the door and drew the curtains. Sonny tried to block out the thumping and thudding sounds from outside. He didn't want to think about what kind of monsters might be flinging themselves against the doors and windows. Or how long it would be before they found a way inside.

"Basement," Mr. Chu said. "Now!"

The kids were too tired and too confused to protest. Sonny let himself imagine that, finally, here was a grown-up who could take control of things and tell them what to do. Even if that grown-up was Mr. Chu.

Once they were in the basement, Mr. Chu locked the door behind them. The lock looked pretty flimsy. So did the door.

"I just wanted a little Halloween fun," Mr. Chu said, eyes wild with panic. "I was trying to outdo last year, and, well . . ." He lowered his voice to a hushed whisper. "I think I brought Halloween to life."

"You didn't, Mr. Chu," Sam said.

"We did." As Sonny said it, the full weight of guilt settled over him. *We did this.* All of it. "We found this manuscript written by this guy, R.L. Stine . . ."

Mr. Chu's face lit up like a light bulb. His head started bobbing up and down with excitement.

"Wait, you mean Robert Lawrence Stine?" he squealed. "The greatest young adult horror author of all time?"

"Clearly you're a fan," said Sarah.

Sonny pressed on. "Anyway, when we opened it, the story came to life."

"Let me get this straight," Mr. Chu said. He looked more amazed by the name R.L. Stine than he had by the fact that his Halloween decorations came to life. "We're living in a *Goosebumps story*? Right now?" He said it like it was good news.

Sarah shook her head. "I know, right? Why couldn't we have gotten stuck in *The Fault in Our Stars*?"

"This is the coolest thing I have ever heard!" Mr. Chu exclaimed. "Which story is it? Don't tell me. Let me guess. *Monster Blood*? No, too on the nose. *The Headless Ghost*? *The Scarecrow Walks at Midnight*?"

"*Slappy Halloween*," Sonny said, deflated. There was no point in hoping that Mr. Chu, of all people, could save them.

"I don't know that one," Mr. Chu said, confused. "How does it end?"

"That's the problem," Sarah said. "It doesn't."

"My mind is literally blown right now," Mr. Chu said, as if Sarah had given him *good* news. "We get to finish our own Goosebumps story? Do you know how cool that is?"

Sonny sighed. They were trapped in the basement with a lunatic.

"This isn't a creative writing exercise, Mr. Chu," Sarah reminded him, more patient than Sonny could have been. "Slappy has our *mom*."

"Well then, you have to save her," Mr. Chu said. "Chapter nineteen, the kids save their mom from the demonic dummy! How do they it?" He scratched his chin, furrowed his brow. "Got it! They use the invisible mirror from R.L. Stine's cautionary classic *Let's Get Invisible!* You make yourselves invisible, sneak into the lab—"

"We don't have an invisible mirror," Sonny pointed out.

Mr. Chu was undaunted. "Okay. Plan B. *The Cuckoo Clock of Doom*, Stine's time travel masterpiece. You set the clock back to before you brought Slappy to life. It strikes the hour. Cuckoo! Cuckoo!" He started flapping his elbows and pecking at the air like a demented bird.

"We don't have a cuckoo clock, either," Sarah said. "The only thing we had was the book. And I lost it."

Sonny glanced sharply at his sister. "Sarah, this isn't your fault," he assured her. It hadn't even occurred to him that she would feel guilty about that. She'd done everything she could to protect them. She'd been a *hero*. How did she not know that?

"I lost the book, Sonny," Sarah said. She slumped against the wall. "Mom trusted me to take care of you guys. She trusted me to save her. And . . . I let her get taken away."

Sonny didn't know what to say. He was the little brother; she was the big sister. His whole life, she'd been there, bossing him around, telling him what to do. Taking care of him. Making him feel better. She was the one who always knew what to say and what to do when things went wrong. How could he convince her that none of this was her fault?

All of it was his fault.

"I know I always say I want to get out of here so I can start my 'real life,' but you and Mom *are* my life," Sarah told him. "I guess sometimes, I focus on what I want, and I forget about what I already have."

For the first time in many years, Sonny wanted to give his sister a hug. Before he could, Mr. Chu bounded in between them. "*Classic* Goosebumps moment!" he cried, pumping his fist. "Just like when Michael Webster realizes that he's erased his little sister from existence. Exactly what he always wanted . . . or was it? Scholars will argue, but I say—"

"This is real life, Mr. Chu!" Sam snapped. "Sarah, please continue. You were about to express your feelings for me, as well . . ."

"Um, nope." Sarah shook her head firmly. "Don't think I was."

Sonny decided there was only one way to wipe that hopeless, guilty look off of his sister's face. This wasn't about finding the right words. This was about making a *plan*.

They had to act, and fast. "Slappy's using the lab to power Halloween," he said. Sonny knew that lab better than anyone. He'd been obsessed with it his entire life. He'd learned everything there was to know about Tesla. He'd studied the floor plans. And . . . he realized he knew how Slappy's power supply worked.

He'd built a tower of his own, based precisely on Tesla's design—which meant he knew how to power it up. And how to power it *down*. "If we can get inside, I can turn it off. We can save Mom."

"One problem," Sam said. "There are monsters everywhere. How are we gonna get past them?"

Sarah turned slowly toward Mr. Chu. A smile crept across her face. "Camouflage," she said.

After a beat, Sonny caught on. So did Mr. Chu, who loved the idea. He led them over to a corner of the basement shielded by a floor-to-ceiling curtain. With a magician's flourish, he drew it back, revealing a full-scale costume workshop. Makeup table, sewing machine, fabrics, paints, beads, wigs. Everything they could possibly need to make themselves into monsters.

Mr. Chu giggled. "Am I the only one getting goosebumps?"

* * *

Slappy had his new mother right where he wanted her. Bound, gagged, and chained to a metal chair in the center of the laboratory.

"Hello, Mama." He waved at Kathy Quinn. She blinked helplessly back at him, a pleading look in her eyes. "Remember me?" Slappy said. "You put me on your lap, put those cute words in my mouth. What was it you called me? Bobo?"

Kathy tried to speak, but the gag muffled her words. Good. Slappy was tired of listening to humans talk. Tonight was the dummy's turn.

"What's that?" Slappy said. "Can't talk? Don't worry. From now on, I'll do the talking for the both of us. I'm gonna make you so proud, Mama."

Kathy shook her head wildly and struggled against the chains, but it was no use. Slappy wrapped his wooden fingers around a heavy lever and switched it on.

Electric current flowed into the chair. His new mother twitched and stiffened as the current sizzled through her. She was almost ready. So was Slappy.

He closed his eyes. Raised his arms. Recited his incantation—backward. *"Onarrak Unolom Amol Annodo Irram Urrak . . ."*

Very soon now, his new family would be complete.

CHAPTER 20

Sonny turned himself into a jack-o'-lantern. Sam dressed as a skeleton. Sarah draped herself with a black cloak and donned a green witch's mask. They were three monsters, ready to battle the night.

Mr. Chu, wrapped tightly in his mummy costume, followed them out of the house. "Play it cool, kids."

Unfortunately, he didn't take his own advice. Still overexcited by the thought of being in a Goosebumps story, Mr. Chu gave a little leap as he stepped onto the porch and bumped his head against the doorframe. Which knocked his mummy bandages askew. Which revealed his all-too-human face.

Which had every single mummy in the yard turning slowly in his direction, ready to attack. They approached from all sides.

He ran.

"Don't worry about me!" Mr. Chu screamed over his shoulder, bandages unwrapping themselves as he dashed

across the lawn. "I'll distract them! Save your mom! Save our town! Finish the story!"

The mummies followed him down the block. A swarm of bats swooped past, hot on their tail.

"He'll be okay, right?" Sam asked the others.

"He will be, if we can shut that tower down," Sonny said. "If not . . ."

No one wanted to think about what would happen then.

Sarah had never been so grateful for her beat-up old station wagon. The costumes got them safely to the car. And once inside, they made it to the edge of town without having to fight any more monsters.

Unfortunately, now they'd reached Tesla's lab, where they were going to have to face Slappy, the biggest monster of all.

"We're really here!" Sonny said, peering at the laboratory complex in awe. "It's even cooler up close."

"Hey, fanboy." Sarah snapped her fingers in front of his nose. *"Focus."*

Someone—or, more likely, some*thing*—had ripped a gaping hole in the barbed wire fence surrounding the property. Sarah and the boys ducked through it, then crept silently toward the central laboratory building. They reached a tall, gray, metal door, and hesitated. Sarah gave it a tug: unlocked.

She glanced at the boys, asking a silent question. They both nodded. This was it. They were going in.

The building smelled old. Ancient. Lights flickered. Rust coated the walls. Mold sprouted from the ceiling. Sarah could hear the steady whir of the turbine, and the soft hum of electric current. The air felt strange, too thick. Her skin tingled. She pressed a palm to the back of her neck: goosebumps.

"Take these," Sonny said, handing Sam and Sarah each a small light bulb. "They'll help us find the main turbine. The closer we get, the brighter they'll burn. If we can find the main power source, we can turn the tower off."

"So glad our life depends on your botched seventh-grade science project," Sarah said.

Meanwhile, in the center of town, an ancient Jeep Wagoneer screeched to a stop outside the post office. Slowly, the driver's side door opened, and a stout, middle-aged man dressed in chinos, a V-neck cardigan, and horn-rimmed glasses stepped out.

It was R.L. Stine.

Stine looked around despairingly as witches streaked over his head. He took a step back as a police car with blaring sirens whizzed by.

The Headless Horseman was chasing a few townspeople in the opposite direction from the police car.

"Oh, no . . ." Stine breathed. "Not . . . not this . . ."

A young man almost knocked Stine over as he fled from an inflatable lawn ghoul. Its power cord was trailing behind it.

Stine looked embarrassed. "Oh, my writing was so cliché back then . . ."

He turned around slowly, taking in the full scene. Until his eyes fell on the Wardenclyffe Lab tower in the distance. The top of the tower was sparking with electricity.

Stine gasped. "That clever dummy is writing his own ending!" A look of determination crossed his face. "Not on my watch, he's not."

He turned back to the Wagoneer. A lone lawn gnome blocked his path. It raised a tiny but sharp-looking scythe and began marching toward Stine.

"Oh, gnome . . ." Stine sighed.

The lawn gnome was getting closer. "Don't you dare! Sit. Stay!" Stine cried.

The tiny scythe slashed at his pant leg.

"Darn it!" Stine said. He lifted one foot and stomped it on the gnome's jaunty little cap, crushing it. Then he kicked away the pieces and hurried back to the Wagoneer.

"No wonder Tesla abandoned this place," Sam complained as he and Sonny and Sarah slogged through a puddled hallway. It smelled like something had crawled into the shadows and died—a long, long time ago.

Sonny led the way, Sarah and Sam tiptoeing single file behind him. Without warning, Sonny stopped cold. Sarah nearly toppled into him. "Oh my god!" he said, in a loud whisper.

"What?" Sarah asked in alarm.

Sonny held his glowing light bulb up to a strange, rusting piece of machinery. It was intricately covered with dials, levers, and probes. To Sarah, it looked like a piece of junk. But Sonny was running his hands over it, gently and carefully, as if he'd found an impossibly fragile treasure.

"It's Tesla's sectorless static electricity influence machine," he breathed. "Look at that original rivet work. It's even more beautiful than the pictures."

Sarah hadn't known it was possible to be this exasperated and this proud all at the same time.

"It's getting brighter," she said, showing Sonny her glowing bulb. "This way."

They hesitated at the foot of a crumbling staircase. Sarah could hear someone moving around up there. Which meant they were closing in.

It also meant she really, really wanted to run as fast as she could in the opposite direction. But she couldn't abandon her mother. Not when it was her fault that her mother was here in the first place.

At least, she hoped her mother was here.

They climbed. Step by step. When they reached the top, they discovered themselves at the threshold of the main laboratory. Tesla's own laboratory, crowded with orbs, turbines, transmitters—all of them crackling with electricity.

There was a large, metal chair at the center of the room, like something you'd see in a doctor's office. There was someone in it. Sarah could only see the back of the person's head, but it was a very familiar back.

"Mom!" she cried.

The three kids ran heedlessly into the room and crowded around Kathy—and then froze in horror.

Sarah and Sonny's mother's face had been transformed into the face of a wooden dummy.

CHAPTER 21

"Isn't this nice?" Slappy said from his perch on Kathy's lap. *"A family reunion."*

Horrified, Sarah couldn't take her eyes off her mother. Her wrists were bound to the chair, her eyes glazed and blank, her jaw wooden, hinged, and painted with a blood-red smile. "What did you *do*?" Sarah cried, barely able to choke out the words.

"My first great invention." Slappy gave his prisoner a cheerful poke. She didn't react. *"I call her Mama. I had a papa once. He let me down. But a mother's love is forever. But don't take my word for it . . . Mama?"*

Sarah felt like she was going to puke. Her mother's jaw swiveled open—and Slappy's voice came out. *"You're the greatest son a mother could ever have, Slappy."*

"Oh, *shucks*," Slappy said. *"You don't have to say that."* Then he started to cackle. *"Actually, yeah, you do."*

As Slappy laughed harder, their mother began to laugh, too, with Slappy's maniacal giggle. Her shoulders shook in time with the dummy's.

"He's doing a ventriloquist routine with your *mom*," Sam said, his voice shaking.

"Impressed?" Slappy asked. *"Not even moving my lips."*

"Turn our mom back, now!" Sonny ordered him.

"Don't you mean our *mom?"* Slappy grinned. Sarah wished she still had that shovel so she could whack the stupid evil grin off of his stupid evil face. *"I'm teaching you a lesson about family. Now that mine is complete, I'm going to make certain it's never taken from me again."*

Sarah noticed someone lurking in the corner. It was an ogre—who looked suspiciously like Walter, the cashier from Walgreens.

That's when—even though things seemed like they couldn't get any worse—things got worse. Slappy reached under the chair and pulled out R.L. Stine's unfinished manuscript.

"Give me the book, Slappy," Sarah said.

"No can do, sis!" The dummy sounded disgustingly cheerful. And why not? He was right: He had everything he wanted.

"I'm finally going to do what Stine couldn't. I'm going to finish this book—and write an ending that never ends," the dummy rasped. *"Spoiler alert: The book gets destroyed and Halloween lasts forever!"* He tucked the book under his arm, hopped off their mother's lap, and hurried off into the shadows.

"Where'd he go?" Sam asked.

As if in answer to his question, the room shook with a loud, mechanical creaking noise, like the grinding of metal on metal. The roof was peeling itself open. One by one, the stars poked through.

A deafening whirr kicked in. It was coming from the tower. Slappy had boarded a construction elevator and was riding it all the way to the top.

"Mama, babysit the children for me!" he cried down at them.

Sarah's mother opened her mouth. Slappy's own voice came out. *"Yes, dear."*

Sarah shuddered. "Sonny, turn this tower off. I'm going after that book."

She didn't want to leave her brother and Sam alone with . . . with the horrible *thing* that Slappy had turned her mother into, but she didn't see any other choice.

As she rushed out of the room, the ogre came toward her. She body-checked him, and he stumbled backward, tripping over something on the floor and knocking himself out. Sonny and Sam stared in shock.

Sarah ran to the base of the tower. The elevator had only a single car, which Slappy had claimed for himself. But there was a narrow, rickety stairwell that wound around the narrow tower, all the way up to the top. It looked terrifying.

Sarah shrugged off her fear and began to climb.

"It's just me and you now, Slappy!" she shouted up at the dummy. He had a huge lead, but she would catch up with him. She had to.

129

*   *   *

Even with a dummy's mouth, even speaking with Slappy's voice, this was still his mother, Sonny thought. Surely he could get through to her. "Mom, listen to me." He looked her straight in the eyes, willed her to remember herself. "You need to help us stop Slappy."

His mother just stared at him with that creepy blank gaze, and responded with Slappy's low, cruel voice. *"Oh, honey, I can't play favorites."*

The worst part was when she smiled.

"Dude, how do we turn her off?" Sam asked.

"I think if we can shut down the tower we can turn her back to normal," said Sonny. He pointed at a wall covered with a maze of circuits, dials, and switches. He and Sam approached it.

"This is so much more complicated than my school project," Sonny groaned. He began studying the board from top to bottom.

A few minutes later, he was just as lost as he'd been when he first spotted the wall of circuits.

"This is taking too long," Sam said. "Let's just start unplugging stuff."

"No!" Sonny cried. "If you pull the wrong wire, it'll create an electrical current through your body. It'll kill us!" He stared at the wall. "Slappy really messed with all this stuff."

"*Now, dear, if you can't say anything nice about your brother, then don't say anything at all,*" his mom said in a fake-sweet voice.

"Mom, please!" said Sonny. He turned his attention back to the wall of wires.

"*But, sweetheart . . .*" his mom began.

"Mrs. Quinn!" Sam said. "I don't mean to be rude, but shut your trap!"

Sonny took a deep breath, crossed his fingers for luck, then grabbed a yellow wire, and pulled.

Zap!

A bright spark, a jolting electric shock, then nothing. The turbines continued to whir. The current continued to flow.

"Well, that didn't do anything," Sonny said, disappointed in himself.

"Try that one!" Sam said.

Sonny flipped a switch. "Nothing," he sighed.

Since his back was to his mom, Sonny didn't realize that he had, in fact, accomplished something.

The shackles binding Kathy Quinn to her chair had slipped open. She freed herself, stood up, and walked stiffly toward her son.

CHAPTER 22

Sarah was at least a hundred feet up in the air when she heard something climbing behind her. She had a sinking feeling that she probably didn't want to look down.

But she did anyway. A silvery strand of spiderweb wrapped itself around the stairwell, a few stories beneath her. And scrambling up it was Mr. Chu's twenty-foot-wide balloon spider. It stabbed a balloon leg in her direction.

Sarah ducked around the stairwell, nearly losing her balance. The spider shot another strand of web straight at her. She jumped out of its way, and the silver web sailed past her head, sticking *splat* against Slappy's elevator car.

The lift jolted to a stop, still several feet away from the top of the tower.

The spider screamed with frustration as Sarah kept dodging its attacks. She tempted it closer and closer to the electric blasts spurting from the tower, until it waved a balloon leg a little too close to the power. *ZZZZZAAAAAP.* A spark of static electricity leaped from the tower to the spider, and an entire leg of balloons exploded.

The spider shrieked. Sarah climbed. Far above her, Slappy hoisted himself out of the elevator car and began to scramble up the side of the tower with his little wooden feet.

"Come on, Sonny," Sarah murmured, willing her brother to hurry. "Turn this thing off."

She was gaining on Slappy, but not fast enough.

Sonny had tried one wire after another. The good news was, he had managed not to electrocute himself. The bad news was, the current was still flowing into the tower, and he was no closer to finding the main circuit breaker than he'd been when he started.

"I can't do it," Sonny admitted. He was on the verge of giving up. "I don't know how. This is *Tesla*. I'm only in the seventh grade!"

Sam put a hand on his shoulder. "But you're the smartest kid in the seventh grade," he argued. "Even though you blew up the entire classroom. You got this."

That was exactly Sonny's problem. How could he be expected to make the right decision here when he hadn't even managed to get a tiny model of the tower working?

All those weeks he'd spent fiddling with it, all the effort he'd put in trying to perfect it, and all it had taken was one tweak from Slappy to turn it into an electrified disaster. Total meltdown!

Suddenly, Sonny's brain lit up like a light bulb. *Total melt-down* . . . that was it!

"You're right," Sonny said. "The classroom!"

"What?" Sam wasn't following. But he would.

"We can't turn this thing off," Sonny explained. He pointed Sam to the heavy lever toward the edge of the wall, which Sonny had traced to one of the main power lines. "But we can turn it *up*. Grab that lever."

Sonny took hold of a second lever, which, he was pretty sure, amped the power to the main turbines. "We can push them up at the same time and short out the system."

Sam looked skeptical. "You sure?"

Sure was possibly an overstatement. Sonny thought it *might* work? Possibly?

Before he could admit this, he heard a voice behind him. Slappy's voice.

"Boys, let's not touch things that don't belong to us."

Sonny looked slowly over his shoulder. It wasn't Slappy, of course.

It was his mother.

"How'd she get out of the chair?!" Sam cried.

"Sitting all day isn't good for your lumbar," Kathy said menacingly.

"Mom, listen to me, we're going to save you, okay?" Sonny said desperately. "But just stay back." He turned to Sam. "When I tell you, push that lever, and I'll push this one at the same time."

"Not now, kids," Mom said. *"Let go or you'll be grounded . . . for the rest of your lives!"*

"Trust me," Sonny told Sam. It was now or never. He gripped the lever. Sam did the same. They locked eyes. They would have to do this at exactly the same time, or it wouldn't work.

"No, don't!" his mother screamed, reaching for him.

"Now!" Sonny shouted, and both boys pushed the levers up as far as they could.

The room lit with electric sparks. Smoke sputtered. Current spurted. The dials along the ceiling redlined. An alarm began to wail. Every bulb exploded in a shower of glass.

It was working!

"Hang on, Sarah!" Sonny screamed up to the tower.

The floor shuddered beneath them. The walls shook.

"Mom, get down!" Sonny shouted, as chunks of plaster dropped from the ceiling. It was as if the entire lab was falling to pieces.

So was Mrs. Quinn, her personality bouncing back and forth with the current. *"Mommy doesn't live here anymore!"* she shouted in the dummy's voice. Then, suddenly, she spoke in her own. "Sonny, I'm so sorry."

"Mom?"

"Lights out, brats!" she shouted, Slappy-like again. Then, mom-like, "Are you okay?"

"Mom, it's *me*," Sonny said, grabbing her shoulders and shaking her. "Slappy turned you into a dummy."

"Who you calling dummy?" Her hands closed around his wrists, iron tight. She squeezed until it hurt. Her gaze was once again blank and cold. *"Dummy."*

At that moment, the floor heaved, and something deep beneath them gave a mighty rumble. Then the ceiling caved in.

CHAPTER 23

Sarah felt as if she'd been climbing for hours. She was only a couple of flights beneath Slappy—but that was still too far. He pulled himself onto the platform at the very top of the tower. The sparking bolts of electricity made him look even more demonic than usual. Sarah craned her neck as she climbed, trying to keep him in sight. What was he planning?

Slappy held the book over his head like a trophy. *"And so Slappy merged science with fiction, destroying the manuscript with the same energy that brought the story to life!"*

Sarah's heart leaped into her chest. Energy surged through her and she raced up the last two flights. She could *not* let him destroy that book.

Slappy approached the shooting beam of current running through the center of the tower and up into the clouds. He was going to incinerate the book.

She was so close. Just one more step, and—

Gotcha. Sarah clamped a hand around Slappy's ankle and

yanked as hard as she could. The dummy slammed backward onto the landing. The book dropped out of his hand.

Sarah lunged for it and felt her hands close over the weathered leather. "It's time for you to go back where you belong," she told Slappy, flipping the book open.

At least, she tried to flip it open. Slappy trained his psychic powers on the leather cover, holding it closed. Sarah tried to force it, but the book was welded shut.

"What's the matter?" Slappy taunted. *"Writer's block? Again?"*

"That is *low,*" Sarah said, her fury giving her new strength. She tugged harder at the book, and felt it give just a little.

"I'm twenty-eight inches tall," Slappy bragged. *"You have no idea how low I can go. But you're about to find out."*

"Sonny! What's happening?" Kathy asked. She was back to normal. For now.

"Mom!" Sonny grabbed her hand. "Come on, Sam, we need to get out of here."

Dodging debris and plaster, Sonny, Sam, and Kathy ran blindly through the smoke, and made it out of the room just before the roof collapsed.

But then Sonny's mother started racing toward the stairs as she looked toward the top of the tower.

Sonny and Sam chased after her. The walls were shaking around them. This whole place was about to go down.

They took the tower stairs three at a time. As Sonny paused to catch his breath, he peered up into the night. Far, far above, at the tip of the tower, he could make out his sister. She had hold of the book—but the evil dummy had hold of her.

Sonny couldn't tell who was winning. But if they didn't make it off that tower before the whole complex went up in smoke, everyone was going to lose.

Sarah twisted backward as a nearby transformer spit out a shower of sparks. Something was happening, something big. The narrow platform she was balanced on shuddered and rattled, and the beam of light spurting from the tower seemed like it was getting brighter and brighter. *What did you do, Sonny?* she thought.

A second later, the transformer exploded.

Sarah shrieked and ducked for cover. When she looked up, Slappy was there, his ugly grin only inches from her face.

"Don't you know the rules of writing?" Slappy jeered. *"Every story has a beginning, middle, and—"*

A beam of pure energy blazed up from the laboratory, into the sky, burning a pathway through the night—and straight through the center of the tower platform.

"And a twist," Sarah said, finishing Slappy's lesson for him as she kicked the evil doll in its wooden stomach as hard as she could.

With an angry *oof*, Slappy flew backward . . . straight into the crackling energy beam. He hung for a moment, suspended in midair by the electric field, his body shaking, his eyes bulging, his mouth open in a silent scream.

Slappy's head twisted slowly in a full circle, then spun faster and faster, until he became a blur of energy, almost indistinguishable from the beam. Then, with a blinding, angry burst of light, he was blasted into nothingness.

Sarah had about ten seconds to celebrate before a rustling below reminded her that she still had a giant balloon spider to deal with. A balloon spider that had just watched one of its legs explode. It was angry, and it reared back, lifted one of its remaining legs, and tried to impale her.

Sarah opened the book, hoping its magic would still work and suck the spider back in, but the book tugged at her hand. The beam of light—it was exerting some kind of force on the manuscript, trying to drag it out of her hands!

Sarah held tight. She wasn't about to lose this book a second time, not when she was *so* close. The book pulled and pulled toward the beam.

Then something unexpected happened—the *beam* began to pull toward the book. Electric sparks rained down on its pages, which fluttered with a mysterious wind. The binding glowed red-hot, burning Sarah's hands.

She held on.

WHOOOOOOOOOSH!

Finally, the book worked its magic, and the gigantic spider was sucked away for good. But instead of dying away, as it usually did, the magical wind only intensified. It became a

cyclone, churning the air around the tower and expanding outward.

Soon the whole town was swept up in its power. From miles away, Halloween monsters were whisked off the ground and sucked toward the book. The sky filled with shrieking, flailing beasts.

Mummies, skeletons, bedsheet ghosts, gummy bears, jack-o'-lanterns, abominable snowmen, witches . . . every single demonic creature Slappy had brought to life was jerked off the ground, into the clouds, drawn inexorably into the heart of the whirlwind. Until finally, one by one by one, they were sucked into the pages of the book.

WHOOOOOOSH.

WHOOOOOOSH.

WHOOOOOOSH.

POP.

Silence.

Even the energy beam had been sucked into the book.

The night was perfectly still. Sarah waited, unable to believe it was actually over. She scanned the tower beside her, the sky around and above her. She saw only the stars, the clouds, and far, far below, Sonny and Sam and her mother, waving frantically for her to come down.

Sarah limped down, finally joining her family in the ruined laboratory.

"Halloween is officially over," she said, scooping Sam and Sonny into a relieved hug.

There was only one question left.

"Mom?" Sonny said, looking nervously at his mother.

Sarah held her breath. Their mother's face had gone back to normal, but there was no telling what lived inside her head. What if some shred of Slappy remained?

"Kids?" their mother said, in a familiar, if befuddled voice. Sarah let out a *whooooosh* of her own that was pure relief.

"What is going on?" their mother asked. "All I remember is feeling like I lost you forever . . . and now I can barely move my jaw."

Sarah opened her arms, and now all four of them embraced tightly. She'd never felt so safe and comforted. She never wanted to let go.

"We saved you," said Sarah.

Kathy looked confused. "You saved me? From what?"

Just then, the door to the laboratory burst open. A stout man in horn-rimmed glasses and a V-neck cardigan stood there, clutching a battered old typewriter, sweating profusely from exertion. He looked as if he'd just run a marathon.

"I'm here! Do not worry!" he exclaimed. "Everything is going to be okay. I'm going to need typing paper, an extra ribbon, correction tape, a thesaurus, Diet Coke, and a quiet place to write—preferably someplace with a sturdy chair and good lumbar support . . ."

Sarah, Sonny, and Sam looked at one another in confusion.

"Um . . . are you R.L. Stine?" Sarah finally asked.

"No, I'm Dr. Seuss. R.L. Stine wasn't available," he replied sarcastically. "Yes, of course I'm R.L. Stine!"

Sarah smiled and held out the charred remains of the book. "Then I guess this belongs to you."

Before he touched it, she quickly added, "Don't open it!"

Stine gingerly took the book from her. "My first book," he said, his voice filled with awe. "I was fifteen when I wrote it. Living right here in your town. It's more of an amateur work, really. Although I'm sure you'll agree it shows the undeniable promise of a brilliant young writer."

"Um . . . why are you carrying a typewriter?" Sonny interjected.

Stine looked a little self-conscious. "I was going to save you with it. But apparently you found a way to save yourselves. Which I must admit is very impressive . . ."

Sam was giving Stine his most skeptical look. "Wait, you were gonna save us with a typewriter?"

Now Stine looked fully embarrassed. "It's worked once before . . . maybe twice."

Behind them, a man cleared his throat. "Uh, Kathy?"

It was Walter, climbing out of a heap of rubble. He no longer looked like an ogre—but he did look like a rumpled, burned shirt that could use a good wash and iron.

"Hi," their mother said, blinking in confusion, as if she couldn't quite place him.

Walter tapped his name tag, which was, remarkably, still intact. "Walter. Manager at Walgreens?" he reminded her. "Hi, kids."

"Right. I know. But . . . what are you doing here?" she asked him.

"I don't know," Walter admitted.

"Dude, you got turned into a monster!" Sam exclaimed. "You were Slappy's henchman—"

R.L. Stine cut him off. "Just weather patterns. Very unusual weather patterns. Everything is back to normal now," he said reassuringly.

"Who's this guy?" Walter asked.

"I'm not exactly sure . . ." Kathy replied.

Sarah couldn't help noticing the way her mom and Walter were looking at each other. She wondered if this might be the beginning of a beautiful friendship. Or at least a coffee date. She smiled. Then she caught Sonny's eye and gestured toward the door.

Together, Sarah, Sonny, Sam, Kathy, Walter, and R.L. Stine threaded their way back to the parking lot. Sarah slowed her pace, letting Walter and her mother walk ahead.

"It's so funny running into you," said Walter.

"Right?" said Kathy. "I've always kind of hoped we might see each other outside of Walgreens."

Finally, they all reached the barbed wire fence and, one by one, crawled through the giant hole. Sarah took a deep breath. She knew it was her imagination, but the air smelled fresher on this side. It smelled like home.

"Well, looks like Mom's happy," Sonny said.

Sarah turned to Stine. "So they don't remember what happened to them?"

"No," Stine replied. "The transmutation process appears to have wiped their memories clean. Those who were affected won't remember a thing."

Sam shook his head. "This is officially the craziest day of my life."

Sarah looked up, marveling at how calm and clear the sky was when only a few minutes ago, it had been on fire with monsters.

She was just in time to see a giant creature hurtling down toward her.

CHAPTER 24

Sarah, Sonny, and Sam dove aside into the bushes. The creature slammed into the ground, so hard it kicked up a mushroom cloud of dirt. As the cloud dispersed, they peeked cautiously through the branches, wondering what it could be. A witch, a ghost, some other nasty creature Slappy had left behind?

It was a nasty creature all right.

"Oh my god," Tommy Madigan said, brushing himself off. "I had a crazy dream. You guys were in it. I got taken away by these ladies and was flying around for hours." He paused, then looked at Sonny and Sam. "I'm so glad to see you." He launched himself at Sam and Sonny. Before they knew what was happening, he'd pulled them into an enormous bear hug.

"I can't believe I'm saying this," Sam mumbled, squashed beneath Tommy's thick arm. "But I'm glad to see you, too."

Sarah laughed softly to herself. It wasn't how she'd expected this day to end, but then, nothing about this day had turned out as she'd expected. Since that morning, which felt like a thousand years ago, she'd dumped a zombie boy-friend, destroyed an evil dummy, and saved the world.

And now she was standing next to a world-famous writer.

It was too good an opportunity to pass up. "I'm a writer, too," she told Stine shyly. "Well . . . an aspiring writer—and a very stuck writer at the moment."

Stine shook his head. "My condolences. All the horrors in the world don't come close to the terror of a blank page."

Sarah laughed. "That's true. Any advice on college essays?"

"What's the topic?" Stine asked.

"Tell about a fear you overcame," Sarah replied.

Stine smirked. "Well, you know the first rule of writing: Write what you know." They were close to where he'd left the Wagoneer, and Stine popped the trunk and carefully placed his typewriter inside. Then he looked back at Sarah and smiled. "Thirty years and I couldn't figure out how this book should end. You managed to finish it in one night. I believe in you!"

Then he shook her hand and climbed into his Wagoneer.

As she watched Stine drive away, Sarah smiled. "Who says nothing cool ever happens in this town?"

Then she headed home with her family, eager to see what would happen next.

150

*　　*　　*

Tell about a time in your life when you faced a fear, challenge, or failure.

Sarah stared at the blank screen. It didn't scare her anymore.

These days, not much did.

She typed: *I'm pretty sure you wouldn't believe me if I told you, but what I believe is that we're all afraid. We face different fears, each and every day, whether it's answering questions about ourselves that may determine our future, or being afraid to tell the people we love how much we care. And as scary as it is, you just put one foot in front of the other. You act brave until, one day, you are brave.*

When she'd finished the essay, she spell-checked it one last time, uploaded it to the application, and sent it in.

Then she waited.

Weeks and weeks passed. Sonny won a science award. Her mom and Walter started dating. Sam somehow convinced Tommy to work for the Junk Bros (for free).

Leaves fell from trees, the days grew shorter, the air grew colder, and still, Sarah waited.

Then, just before Christmas, as Sarah pulled into her driveway, her cell phone dinged. It was an e-mail—an e-mail from the Columbia University admissions office. Her finger hovered over the screen, but she couldn't open it yet.

She was afraid.

Mr. Chu waved at her from his porch, where he was stringing up yet another strand of Christmas lights. He was still in a half-body cast, but it hadn't stopped him from turning his house into a Christmas wonderland that rivaled Rockefeller Center.

"Tell your fam, house lighting tonight at eight," he reminded her. "Whole neighborhood's coming."

He stuck a giant extension cord plug into a socket, and a full-sized animatronic reindeer jerked to life. Its head swiveled slowly toward Sarah. She shuddered. Holiday decorations still weren't her favorite thing.

"What do you think?" Mr. Chu asked. "I made it life-sized this time. You know . . . just in case."

Sarah laughed. It was a good reminder that she'd faced far graver threats than an e-mail. She pulled out her phone, touched her fingertip to the screen, and stared straight into her future.

Her legs turned to jelly. Her heart pounded. She felt the back of her neck, and yes, there were goosebumps.

Sarah took a few deep breaths, then went into the house. Kathy, Sonny, and Sam looked at her with alarm. She must have had shock written all over her face.

"Honey?" her mother asked. She was putting the finishing touches on the tree. The house was alive with Christmas: nutcrackers in the window, stockings on the mantel, and a bright, sparkling tree that nearly reached the ceiling. "What happened?"

Sarah held up her phone for them to see. Her heart was bursting with joy. "I got in!"

The family exploded with cheers and excitement.

"Don't worry, Sarah," said Sam. "We can do the long-distance thing."

Sarah laughed and rolled her eyes. Then she hugged her mom and Sonny—hard.

Meanwhile, on the shores of a secluded lake in upstate New York . . .

R.L. Stine was flexing his fingers over his typewriter. He had just written the final sentence of his latest story.

Carefully, he removed the last sheet of paper from the typewriter and bound it into a leather-bound book with a brand-new lock. Then he carried it to the bookshelves lining the walls of his rustic cabin. He pressed a button hidden along the side, and the bookshelves slid open, revealing a storeroom filled with charred Goosebumps manuscripts.

Stine examined the shelves for a moment, and then found a nice, clean spot for his newest work. He gently set it down.

"Congratulations, Papa," said a familiar voice from behind him.

Stine froze. It couldn't be . . . could it?

Slowly, he turned around. Slappy was sitting in a wing chair by the fireplace. And he held a brand-new leather-bound manuscript, complete with lock.

"S-Slappy, what are you doing here?" Stine managed to stammer.

"Oh, I've been dabbling in writing myself lately," the wooden dummy replied. *"This one's a real page-turner."*

"Why is that?" Stine asked nervously.

"Oh, Papa, because you're *the main character,"* Slappy replied coyly. He clicked open the manuscript's lock.

There was a *whoosh*, quiet at first, but steadily growing louder. Stine looked down. He was getting sucked into the book!

"NOOOOOOO!" he cried.

But it was too late. A moment later, Stine was gone, and the cabin was quiet once more.

Slappy smiled with satisfaction. *"I hear it's a real* scream."